Praise for

DEMON SONG

"*Demon Song* is a fast-paced exploration of the power of performance and the cost of desire by the queen of thrilling murder mysteries, twisty red herrings, and complex mother-daughter relationships."

AI JIANG, Hugo Award nominee and author of *A Palace Near the Wind*

"Magical and forlorn. Yu deftly blends the fantastical imagery of a classic tale with a modern story of having to grow up too fast, joining elegant theater with familial cycles of pain. *Demon Song* makes your heart ache right to the end."

HAILEY PIPER, Bram Stoker Award®-winning author of *Queen of Teeth*

"*Demon Song* reaches such a high note, a blissful blend of Chinese folklore and Shirley Jackson, reading like *The Haunting of Hill's Opera House*, where phantoms flit on pitches no living organism can continue to read sanely."

CLAY MCLEOD CHAPMAN, author of *Wake Up and Open Your Eyes*

"Utterly addicting and an immediate new obsession. This is the kind of story that consumes you more and more with each page and I couldn't get enough of this darkly gothic, sharp-edged tale of wicked bargains, alluring demons, and desperate longing."

CG DREWS, *New York Times*-bestselling author of *Don't Let The Forest In*

"An appetizingly dark Gothic served dripping in mood and laced with Chinese mythology. Yu's love of theatre sings throughout this musical nightmare."

EDEN ROYCE, Bram Stoker Award®-nominated author of *Hollow Tongue*

"*Demon Song* spreads its lovely darkness through the eerie passageways of an aged Beijing opera house, the perfect setting for its many charms. The horror rises like an aria, the evil is enchanting behind its mask, and Kelsea Yu's haunting prose moves like music to its skin-crawling conclusion. If *House of Leaves* absorbed the best of 1960s Asian horror films and classic weird fiction into its hallways, this poisonous novella could be the marrow of such a strange architecture."

MICHAEL WEHUNT, author of *The October Film Haunt* and *Greener Pastures*

"A Chinese theatre horror with themes of intergenerational trauma and marginalization delivered in haunting, lyrical prose, Kelsea Yu's *Demon Song* resounds with originality and flair. Featuring a historic tale which blends seamlessly into the contemporary narrative like a traditional zhiguai, Yu's white bone spirit beguiles and terrifies. A startling new voice in Asian horror, Yu will undoubtedly feature on future award lists."

LEE MURRAY, five-time Bram Stoker Award®-winning author and editor of *Black Cranes* and *Tortured Willows*.

DEMON SONG

KELSEA YU

TITAN BOOKS

Demon Song
Hardback edition ISBN: 9781835410394
E-book edition ISBN: 9781835410400

Published by Titan Books
A division of Titan Publishing Group Ltd
144 Southwark Street, London SE1 0UP
www.titanbooks.com

First edition: September 2025
10 9 8 7 6 5 4 3 2 1

This is a work of fiction. All of the characters, organizations, and events portrayed in this novel are either products of the author's imagination or are used fictitiously. Any resemblance to actual persons, living or dead (except for satirical purposes), is entirely coincidental.

© Kelsea Yu 2025

Kelsea Yu asserts the moral right to be identified as the author of this work.

No part of this publication may be reproduced, stored in a retrieval system, or transmitted, in any form or by any means without the prior written permission of the publisher, nor be otherwise circulated in any form of binding or cover other than that in which it is published and without a similar condition being imposed on the subsequent purchaser.

A CIP catalogue record for this title is available from the British Library.

EU RP (for authorities only)
eucomply OÜ, Pärnu mnt. 139b-14, 11317 Tallinn, Estonia
hello@eucompliancepartner.com, +3375690241

Designed and typeset in Adobe Aldine by Richard Mason.

Printed and bound by CPI (UK) Ltd, Croydon, CR0 4YY.

For my dad,
who took me to see my first musical

CHAPTER 1

It is when something draws to its inevitable end that we think most about how it began. These past few months, with the days stretching longer, the dogwood in our backyard shedding pale blossoms with the warming of the weather, I've been embroiled in an interminable debate with myself. Should I tell you my tale?

There seems little benefit when you cannot change its ending.

But eventually, those incurably human emotions—selfishness and the desire to be known by the ones we love most—won out.

If only I hadn't put this off so long, I would have brought you along on this trip so that we could spend the day together. Instead, I am hunched over the secretary desk in my hotel room at dawn, writing, to the best of my memory, what transpired that summer. Resisting the pull as long as possible and hoping I haven't left things too late.

CHAPTER 2

The wheels of our suitcases squeaked as Mom and I dragged our last worldly possessions through the tiled streets of Beijing. I was a scrawny sixteen-year-old at the time, trying—and failing—to avoid dwelling on everything we couldn't bring as we fled under the cover of a moonless night. My collection of mugs from every place we'd lived. The pile of books Yí had given me before I'd left Portland. My third-favorite sweater. They were all gone, left behind in the spare apartment of the man who swept Mom off her feet with promises of marriage, moved us to China, took our passports away, and then installed her as his mistress.

"We're almost there, Megan." Mom wiped sweat off her forehead. She had lost her usual primped-to-perfection look; her silky black tresses were stringy with grease, and her wrinkled shift dress hung limply over her bony frame.

"Great." I smacked the mosquito nipping at my neck, crumpling its delicate body. Wiping its guts on my jeans,

I bit back the thoughts that threatened to spill out. I was itchy, I smelled like bus, and I missed Yi. But as always, I was expected to act excited about the next place we'd call home... until Mom fucked everything up again.

"Megan?"

I took a deep breath and turned to look at Mom, whose heavy makeup barely covered the ugly bloom of plum beneath. My gaze lingered on her bruises, and my heart softened. "I'm fine. Just... tired."

"I know. I promise you'll love our new home, though." A note of uncertainty crept into her voice. She frowned and picked up her pace, leading us past gray brick buildings with identical arched doorways and roofs. All the shops were all closed for the night, save for one rowdy bar. Music, laughter, and light spilled from its open doorway.

We rounded a corner, and Mom turned toward me, lips spreading into a grin as she gestured dramatically to the building behind her. Imitating an announcer, she boomed, "Welcome to Huīhuáng Opera House!"

Countless glowing red lanterns illuminated a stunning, multi-storied structure. Black lacquered pillars supported a sloped roof lined with tubular tiles, and beneath it lay a massive red façade carved with softly gilded symbols. A golden phoenix crowned the theater, wings spread over a sign emblazoned with traditional hànyǔ characters.

As the lights flickered, the roof's upturned eaves appeared

to sharpen into a wicked grin, red lips splitting to show off a row of jagged, bloodstained teeth.

When I blinked, it was merely a sloped roof again.

"I don't understand." I grabbed Mom's arm before she could join the horde of strangers pushing their way across the street. "Where are we staying?"

Her smile faltered. "You're so impatient, Megan. Can't you ever go with the flow?"

"Just tell me."

She sighed. "The Opera House has built-in living quarters for the troupe and various staff." She paused. "Including cleaners." Mom pulled her arm away and walked off before I could ask more questions. I scrambled to keep up.

My skin prickled as we neared the entrance. Nestled in among high-rises and modern, boxy buildings, its bright coloring and odd silhouette made it look like something dredged from an ancient past. A shiver ran through me as I stepped over the threshold, feeling like we were about to drop into a world long gone.

Mom freshened her lipstick and twisted her hair into a quick bun before knocking. The door opened to reveal a man with slick black hair and a sharp chin. I sighed. Of course. This must be how we came by our new jobs. He had the same hungry eyes and toothy grin as the rest of them, and his gaze lingered on Mom's exposed cleavage for a beat too long.

At least it wasn't on mine.

"Wēi!" Mom leapt forward to hug the man, whose face morphed into a delighted grin.

"Jiā!" He hugged her back. "You made it!"

I rolled my eyes. So, it began.

When she'd finally let him go, she gestured at me. "Megan, this is Wei, an old friend of mine. Wei, this is my daughter, Megan."

I offered up a half-hearted wave. Wei nodded at me, but his gaze immediately turned back to rest on Mom. I might as well have been a pet she'd brought with her.

Wei and Mom chattered away as he led us inside, and through the narrow hallways. I understood barely enough Mandarin to catch the gist. When I'd been younger, Mom and I would converse regularly in her native tongue. Then, one of her longer-lasting boyfriends accused us of talking shit about him behind his back. After that, we dared whisper in Mandarin only in private. Eventually, we switched permanently to English; it was easier not to have to look over our shoulders constantly.

As we turned a corner, Wei noticed my existence and switched to English, pointing out various restorations that the three-hundred year-old theater had undergone in recent years. "Since your mother was last here, we replaced all the rotting rosewood beams and refinished the entire interior! It was a major ordeal, restoring the colors to their original hue."

Despite myself, I found my curiosity piqued. I reached out to touch a lion the size of my palm; one of many carved relief animals and good-luck symbols lining the wall. "That must have taken forever."

"Four years," he said. "And we still do small repairs here and there." I pictured a line of painters working in unison, using tiny brushes to retouch each animal.

"Āiyā," Mom said as we rounded a corner. "They forgot a spot." She pointed to a strip of peeling paint.

Wei frowned. "No matter how often we repaint certain spots, they keep chipping. Almost as if..." He shook his head. "I'm sure it's nothing. Old buildings are strange."

"Maybe this place is haunted," I said.

Mom gave me a warning look. "Don't joke about things like that." She pursed her lips. "And be mindful of where you wander around here. This theater is bigger than it looks. As cautious and thorough as I'm sure the workers were," she smiled at Wei, "they might have missed a rotten board or two."

I wasn't about to argue with Mom in front of Wei, but I crossed my arms to indicate my displeasure. She was treating me like an errant child when I hadn't done anything wrong. Oblivious, Wei continued playing tour guide. He pointed out the shared bathroom before leading us to our room. Sliding open the screen door, he revealed a small bed, dresser, and floor-length mirror. Though the room was tiny, each piece of furniture matched the décor perfectly. Mom stepped inside, inspecting everything.

"Is there a spare sleeping mat? I don't mind the floor." I

yawned, hoping Wei wasn't too obtuse to take the hint.

"No need." Wei's smile set my teeth on edge. "I arranged for you to have separate rooms."

Mom looked up, startled, her fingers curled around the side of the mirror. "Thank you, but that's not necessary."

He waved a hand. "Don't worry, Jia. It's no trouble at all. Megan is a growing teenager; she will appreciate her own space. These rooms are far too small for two."

"I'd rather share with Mom." I narrowed my eyes, well aware of why Wei wanted Mom to have her own room.

Mom's eyes flicked, indecisive, back and forth between me and Wei. My hand curled into a fist; for once, I wanted her to pick my side. To stand up for us.

When Mom turned toward Wei, her lips settling into an overdone smile, my heart sank. "You're right," she said. "Teenagers need space. Thank you for your generosity, Wei."

I didn't argue. I offered Mom the right assurances and bid her goodnight—everything she wanted to hear. I waited until they had both left before I let my tears fall.

Despite the lumpy mattress, I began to drop off. As my eyelids fluttered shut, I heard a song, otherworldly and beautiful, cut through the hazy in-between. Though I could not understand the words, its melody felt true, as if composed of all the sadness I'd shed into my pillow. And then I was out.

I woke in a dark chamber deep within the body of the Opera House—though how I knew this, I could not say. The air was cold and stale as I sat up, shivering. One by one, candles lit up around me, and in the flickering, uneven light, I saw myself— another me, several feet away—startle. She touched her face as I felt my own fingertips brush my cheek. I turned my head, and there was another me, and another, an endless sea of us stretching into the darkness, all turned in precisely the same way. We stared at each other; parted our lips to speak.

Our mouths were empty cavities; nothing but black, gaping maws.

As we screamed, our jaws opened wider, mouths stretching and expanding. A wild, insatiable hunger tore through me, a sudden ache that felt like burst stitches. And then she was above me. A woman in brilliant white robes, unblinking as she gazed into my eyes. She placed a finger over my lips, and my scream stopped abruptly. I could still feel it pressing against my throat, desperate to be released, but I was powerless to move. Smiling, she slid her fingers into my mouth until her entire hand lay inside; until her probing fingers were in my throat, pulling something out as I gagged and choked.

She yanked, hard and abrupt. Blood and sick ran down her arm, staining her billowing white sleeves as she lifted her hand, palm up to reveal the pale pink muscle, still wriggling, forming soundless, impossible words.

CHAPTER 3

I startled awake, chilled by the memory of last night's dream. In the mirror, I stuck out my tongue, reassuring myself it was intact. Just a nightmare. There was a note beneath my door.

> Breakfast is served in the restaurant near the theater entrance. Wei says you can charge whatever meals you want to his account, but don't take advantage, okay? Take the morning to settle in while I sort out our jobs here. Meet me in front of your room at noon and we'll get lunch. We start work after that.
> Love, Mom

I crumpled up the note and tossed it in a corner.

As I made my way toward the restaurant Wei had pointed out the evening before, I recalled that false smile as he insisted Mom and I sleep in separate rooms. I clenched my jaw, nearly turning back. It was tempting to skip breakfast rather than put myself in his debt—even with something as small as a meal charged to his account.

But, as I reached the restaurant, my stomach growled its demands. I gritted my teeth, ordering a pineapple bun to go. The crackly top crunched satisfyingly with each bite. This, at least, was one thing I loved about living in China: the baked goods were delicious.

With nothing better to do, I set off to explore the Opera House.

Behind the vacant ticket booth, I found a shrine. Shiny gold Buddha figurines sat below a wall of photos—some in grayscale, others in color—of past opera stars. I leaned in to inspect them, marveling at their elaborate costumes. Each actor was wrapped in layers of heavy, patterned fabrics, hair bound up in jeweled headdresses. Pronounced makeup transformed their features. One by one, they stared back at me; black wing-lined eyes set against faces painted in exaggerated patterns.

I paused on a photo featuring a singer clad in white robes and a matching cape, both accented with cobalt blue embroidery. Pom-poms topped her pearled headpiece and two long, thin feathers sprouted from either side of her head, like antlers. As I stared, a memory tried to surface; something familiar about the costume or likeness. She reminded me, vaguely, of the white-robed woman in the previous night's dream, but it was more than that. A recollection from somewhere deep in my past.

Beneath the image, several words were scrawled in messy handwriting—hànyǔ characters with an English translation beneath:

I stared at the photo until my eyes began to water, waiting for the connection. Still, it refused to click, leaving me feeling hollow, like I'd missed something essential.

On my way out, I passed by the ticket booth. Beside it, a giant poster showed two opera performers facing off. One was dressed like the Monkey King. As you might guess, my knowledge of classic Chinese literature was much more limited back then, but even I knew of Sūn Wùkōng. The other was dressed like the singer in the photograph.

A well-worn book sat askew on the ticket booth counter. Curious, I reached for it. As my fingertips brushed the spine, a sudden desire came over me. I wanted that book more than I'd wanted anything in ages. After a surreptitious glance around, I slipped it into my hoodie.

I found a quiet corner to sit in before inspecting the book. It looked ancient, with a battered leather cover and warped, yellowing pages. I flipped through pages of Chinese text, stopping at a spot marked by a postcard with the same image as the opera poster.

THE MONKEY KING AND THE WHITE BONE DEMON

I blinked at the chapter title. Why was this page in English? I checked a few pages back.

It was all in English.

I rubbed my face. Clearly, I needed sleep. Someone—a traveler, maybe—must have left their copy here by accident, along with their souvenir postcard. Of course they'd have it open to the current show; they wanted to learn the story. It made sense.

Well, their loss. I began reading.

The evil, shape-shifting spirit known as Báigǔjīng, the White Bone Demon, was particular in her tastes. A craving thrummed through her skeletal body, from the tips of the long tendrils sprouting like horns on her skull, to the gnarled toes of her clawed feet. She was determined to consume the flesh of Táng Sānzàng, the famed Buddhist monk known to be the reincarnation of a holy being. By doing so, she would gain immortality.

When Baigujing learned that Tang Sanzang and his

three disciples were passing near her mountain, she licked her rouge-lined lips in anticipation of the meal ahead. Her sights were set on the reincarnated monk, but her demon friends might enjoy the flesh of his companions—the infamous Monkey King, Sun Wukong; the pig spirit, Zhū Bājiè; and fish spirit, Shā Wùjìng. Baigujing took the form of a young maiden from the local village, appearing before the four weary travelers with a basket of poisoned fruit.

The grateful monk reached out to select a ripe plum, but one of his companions leapt between him and the demon. Sun Wukong was the only one powerful enough to detect Baigujing's deception. Defending his master, Sun Wukong struck the maiden with his legendary golden-banded staff, a blow hard enough to kill her. As she lay in a pool of blood before them, Tang Sanzang turned to his disciple, fury emblazoning his eyes.

"How could you kill an innocent maiden? You have made a vow to defend me, yet you have used your powers to kill a young girl."

"Master," Sun Wukong pleaded, "she was a demon intent on harming you. I am sure of it."

Tang Sanzang did not believe Sun Wukong. Shamed by his disciple, he buried the girl in the soil and the four companions continued on.

However, Baigujing was too strong to die from one beating. Her fingernails turned black as she dug her way through the soil, taking respite in an underground cavern. As she recovered, she thought of the monk's soft cheeks, of the Monkey King's narrowed eyes. And she planned her next attack.

A song interrupted my reading—a rich falsetto melody accompanied by plucky strings. Curious, I stowed the book away and followed the sounds up a staircase. At the top, I pushed aside yellow silk curtains and slipped through.

I found myself on a side balcony, midway up an exceedingly tall room. Light filtered in from windows above, illuminating the colorful interior. Unlike the building's hallways, which made me vaguely claustrophobic with their low ceilings and the promise of creatures ready to leap out from every corner, everything here was bright and inviting, painted red with green and gold accents.

Below me, empty tables and chairs faced an elevated stage. Lacquered pillars held up a miniature, decorative ceiling, and a red backdrop sat behind, patterned with gold thread.

Onstage, a group of ten or so athletic-looking people lounged, some laughing and chatting in Mandarin as others sang and played music. I tucked myself into a shadow, feeling like a creep as I watched what I figured must be the opera troupe. A guy in a monkey mask with the face cut out, brown fur surrounding his head like a mane, planted a huge, wet kiss on the cheek of another guy holding an oversized pig mask.

As Pig Mask Guy slapped him away, laughing, Monkey Guy sneaked behind a girl playing the lute and started braiding her hair. She ignored him, continuing to strum, until he started waving her braid up and down like an undulating snake. She rolled her eyes and turned to tell him off, but her smirk said she wasn't truly bothered.

Their teasing laughter and camaraderie twisted my insides in a way only reminders of the past could. An ache settled in my heart. I missed karaoke with Yi. I missed our wild rehearsal nights—Yi had somehow convinced me to audition with her for our school's production of *The Addams Family*. I thought of her, and me, and the rest of the cast laughing and gossiping as we wiped globs of makeup off one another's faces. I missed home.

A new voice began singing, dulcet tones rich and beautiful. The chatter died, and I followed everyone's gazes to a girl standing below the stage who looked a few years older than me. With her lacy black blouse, dangly rose-shaped earrings, and expensive-looking handbag, she exuded effortless glamour.

When she was done, the group burst into applause, excited energy roiling through the performers. I drew in a breath. She had to be the lead. She was good. Really good. Good enough to pique my curiosity about *The Monkey King and the White Bone Demon*.

I squinted and leaned forward, trying to make out her features.

"Hēi! Nǐ mílùle ma?"

It took a moment to realize the question, shouted by a performer in a maroon T-shirt, was meant for me. I hadn't realized I'd stepped out of the shadows. I rested my elbows on the balcony rail as I searched for whoever was talking. As an added bonus, it gave me a moment to mentally translate my planned reply into Mandarin.

"She's American," someone said. "Or some other country. Not Chinese."

Not Chinese. The words pitted in my stomach. "Wǒ huì jiāng zhōngwén." I stood up straighter. "Wǒ zài zhè'er dǎgōng."

Two of them exchanged looks. It was difficult to tell which of my claims garnered more of their skepticism: that I could speak Mandarin or that I worked there.

"Sure, sure." Maroon Shirt waved me down. "Come join us, American girl! We can speak English!"

Once upon a time, I would have been too shy to join a group of strangers, especially when they all seemed to know each other intimately. But after countless moves, my nervousness about meeting new people had lessened somewhat, even if I still didn't really enjoy it. I wasn't afraid, though. By then, I'd learned that it's the ones closest to you that you need to be wariest of.

Soon, I was in the heart of the crowd, leaned up against the stage. Up close, I could see that most of the performers weren't much older than me. Proximity accented their muscular bodies, highlighting my own puniness in comparison. Several of them passed a bottle of something that smelled alcoholic between them. Monkey Guy took a swig. From onstage, Maroon Shirt grinned at me. "Was I right? You're American?"

I hadn't yet figured out what gave me away, but everyone in China seemed to be able to pin me down as American right away. "Yeah."

Maroon Shirt slid down the stage, landing in front of me with a thump. I stepped back to avoid a collision. His breath reeked of alcohol. "So, what do you do, American girl?"

"I'm part of the cleaning staff, *Chinese boy*."

One of his friends snickered, but he continued, unfazed. "Okay, okay, I should have introduced myself. I'm Háozhé. What's your name?"

I scooted away before answering. "Megan."

He winked at me. "Well, Megan. You're welcome to hang out with us anytime."

Behind him, one of the performers made a gagging sound. "Don't be gross. She's just a baby."

"I'm sixteen." I'd met his type before. *Not* interested. And attraction worked differently for me than it seemed to for others, anyway.

I turned my back to Haozhe and found myself in the middle of two people entangled in an argument. A burly guy folded his arms, looking at the girl in the lacy black blouse. The one with the beautiful voice.

"There's still time to switch our next play," Burly Guy

said. "Can't you convince your rich fiancé to use his K-pop money to fund a more traditional story?"

Lacy Blouse sighed. "You got the fucking lead role in the next show and you're *still* complaining."

"Exactly. It'll be my name on the posters."

"We've gone over this," she said. "Joon-Ho thinks modernization will help revive interest in the art form. And you know he's right, even if you hate it. Look how well Shanghai Opera House's last show went. Sold out every night for the first month!"

"That's Shanghai," Burly Guy grumbled. "We're the country's capital and guardians of Chinese culture. It's not Beijing opera anymore once we throw in expensive sets that move and light up."

"Not this again." Haozhe stepped between the two, resting his elbows on their shoulders and swinging back and forth between them. "Hey, Megan! What do you think?"

"Oh, I don't..."

"Come on." Haozhe groaned. "We can't listen to them have the same discussion again. We need a neutral opinion! Does modernization ruin an art form?"

"Um... well..." The more I stammered, the more the group's eyes settled on me. Finally, I channeled something Yi had said once. "Every art form has to evolve in some ways to survive. If done tastefully, the new can enhance the old. I think it can be beautiful."

A smile quirked on the girl's face. I felt my heartbeat pick up, a light flush spreading across my cheeks.

Burly Guy turned toward me, breath reeking of alcohol. His lips curled up in a sneer. "Americans think they know better than everyone, don't they? You speak Mandarin like you're in grade two and you know nothing of Chinese opera." He switched from English to Mandarin, words so rapid I had a hard time keeping up. From the expressions on everyone's faces, I could tell that whatever he was saying was meant to insult. I felt myself turn brighter red.

"Hey!" Lacy Blouse said. "Haozhe asked for her opinion. No need to be an asshole, Sìquán." She hopped off the stage. "Megan, was it? I was about to take a break. Join me?"

She shouldered the guy next to me out of the way and headed down the hall. Stunned, I followed her a moment later, relief washing over me as we left. Behind us, chatter resumed, leaving me wondering if arguments like these were normal for the troupe.

In the hallway, Lacy Blouse stopped. "Don't mind Siquan. He has a drinking problem. At this rate, he's going to burn out of theater soon, despite his talent."

"That's... too bad." The words felt inadequate, but I was too shaken to form a more coherent response.

She smiled. "I'm Kristy."

"Oh! That doesn't sound like a Chinese name." I clapped a hand over my mouth. "I'm sorry. I really am a horrible American."

She laughed. "I lived in Canada until I was seven. Have you been to the teahouse yet?"

I followed Kristy down a maze of hallways to the back of the theater, where we entered a cute, traditional-looking teahouse. Inside, we sat at a small table near the back as a server clad in a yellow qípáo took our order. Kristy asked for a steaming pot of oolong, two teacups, and a small plate of cookies for us to share. Rays of sunlight peeked through the windows, lighting her face in a warm glow. I wrapped my hands around my chipped teacup, blowing gently.

"Some of the performers get really touchy about tradition." Kristy sipped her tea, steam clouding her face. The huge diamond ring on her finger sparkled each time she lifted her cup. "Siquan is an arrogant little asswipe, but he also has good reason. His grandfather was a famous opera singer who was killed during the Cultural Revolution." Kristy shook her head. "Chinese opera has been dying out, and Siquan wants to preserve it."

"You don't feel the same way?"

If I hadn't been staring at that exact moment, I would have missed the way Kristy's lips pursed, eyes narrowing nearly imperceptibly. The odd look was gone in an instant.

"My feelings about Chinese opera are complicated," she said at last. "My dad was really into preserving tradition. I think... sometimes things need to be shaken up."

"My dad was, too." As soon as the words were out, my jaw

tightened, as if to keep anything else from escaping. Why had I said that? I never talked about him.

"Was?" There was a softness to Kristy's words, but her eyes bored into mine.

I swallowed. "Yeah. My dad... well, my stepdad, but it never mattered to me, or to him. He loved traditions. Things with a rich history. And he would have loved it here."

Unbidden, a memory filled my mind. Dad—the only one from my childhood who deserved the title—taking us to see *Les Misérables* on a cool summer night. Letting me pick a poster from the theater shop to put up in my room. It stayed on my wall through the fighting and the divorce. Yi was keeping it safe for me while I was in China.

"You lost him?" Kristy asked with that same intensity.

I shrugged. "In a way. We don't talk anymore. After my parents split up, Mom wanted a clean break." I didn't know why I was telling her all that. I'd rarely shared this much with anyone.

Then again, it had been a long time since anyone had cared to ask.

Kristy sat back, looking more relaxed. Or disappointed, maybe. "Losing a parent is hard, no matter how it happens." She took a sip of tea. "My dad is the reason I started singing. It makes me think of him. This opera, especially."

"I haven't seen a Chinese opera yet," I admitted. "But I heard you singing earlier. You have a beautiful voice." I winced. "That sounded weird. I just mean I wish I could sing like you." I kicked myself. That was even worse. I stuffed a cookie in my mouth, hoping it would diffuse my awkward comments.

She cocked her head. "You sing?"

I washed down the crumbly cookie with a sip of oolong. "Not officially or anything. Just for fun. My best friend's really into karaoke. And, um... my family used to be into singing." I tried not to think about Dad again.

"Fun is the best reason to sing." She smiled. "If you ever want some lessons, come find me, alright?"

"Thanks!" I was cynical enough, then, to wonder if she meant it. When you were a nobody, most people thought nothing of breaking promises they'd made to you.

As we finished our tea and cookies, Kristy told me more about the troupe and the theater, warning me who to keep my distance from and who was safe to befriend. She wasn't a fan of Wei, which made me like her even more. Too soon, our plates and cups were empty, and she paid for us both, waving away my half-hearted protests. I was relieved—after our conversation, I was loath for her to find out Wei was covering the bills for Mom and me.

"One more thing," Kristy said as we walked out of the restaurant. "Be careful, okay?" She glanced to the side, as if someone might be listening.

"Careful of what?"

Kristy pursed her lips. She didn't respond immediately. When she finally spoke again, there was a distant look in her eyes. "Just... be careful. This theater has outlived generations of people. Places like this have a history. Desires. And this one is famished."

CHAPTER 4

That night, my muscles ached from an afternoon spent scrubbing bathrooms. Mom only had to clean bedrooms, which seemed unfair, but she was adamant about not switching. At the time, I figured she was worried I'd steal something. I wouldn't have, though it might have been tempting to poke around the performers' rooms a bit.

I stretched and slipped into bed, opening the book to continue reading by lamplight.

When Baigujing had recovered enough, she clawed her way back out of the cavern and through the dirt. She spun a new disguise; this time, she took the form of an old woman. When she approached Tang Sanzang and his disciples, she was displeased to note that the Monkey King was still among them, but she wouldn't let him deter her. Wailing loudly, she approached the group.

Tang Sanzang greeted her. "Pópo, what afflicts you? My

companions and I are at your service."

"My daughter was murdered by bandits! She went to the market to buy fruit for her ailing father. When she did not return, we searched far and wide, eventually coming across her dead body shoved into a hastily dug hole! She was our only child." The old woman resumed sobbing.

The monk grew pale. He turned toward Sun Wukong, expecting contrition and an offer of reparation from the Monkey King. Instead, Sun Wukong leapt forward with his staff and struck the old woman with a fatal blow, the same way he had done with the maiden.

Once again, Tang Sanzang was horrified. "You were meant to accompany me on my quest as redemption for your past sins. Yet, as my disciple, you have now slain two innocent villagers! What have you to say for yourself?"

"Master," Sun Wukong said, "she was a demon in disguise as well. I seek only to keep you safe."

"Next time you fall out of line, I will pronounce the secret words taught to me by the bodhisattva Guānyīn, leaving you in unbearable pain. I do not wish to do so, but you leave me no choice."

After this decree, Tang Sanzang forbade his other two disciples, pig spirit Zhu Bajie and fish spirit Sha Wujing, from speaking with Sun Wukong. In tense silence, they buried the dead woman and continued on their way.

This second injury from the golden-banded staff left

Baigujing further weakened, but her hunger only grew. As she lay recovering, she dreamt of sweet monk's flesh, simmered into a stew.

A yawn escaped my mouth, and I set the book down; I'd pick it up again in the morning. Switching the lamp off, I lay my head down on the pillow, drifting off within minutes.

∽

When I woke again, it was the dead of night. Notes sung in a high-pitched, Chinese operatic voice lifted me from sleep. My thoughts swam through thick air, everything filtering through a mental haze, but the song drew me. I stepped out of bed, following the sound.

The corridor was unevenly lit, flickering candles adding depth to the relief-carved animals on the walls. It should have struck me as odd, but all I felt was awe and curiosity as I ran my fingers along the scales of a sinewy dragon, tracing the whorls of its serpentine body. With each step, cold chilled the soles of my feet, but I kept moving forward. The further I walked, the bigger the hallway seemed, like I was being swallowed up by a cavernous mouth.

The music grew in volume as I neared the auditorium. I pushed through curtains, finding myself in the center aisle. Like the hallway, this room felt impossibly vast, and it was lit mostly by candles. All except the stage, which blazed with lights that shone on a set of performers in full, striking regalia.

The Monkey King wielded his staff, Jīngū Bàng, against a figure dressed in flowing white robes, the two battling in a beautiful sequence. Instinctively, I knew she was the White Bone Demon. Sun Wukong attacked in a series of flips and twirls, spinning Jingu Bang quickly enough for it to blur. Each assault was met with a graceful dodge, Baigujing rolling and cartwheeling away. Their movements were timed with the clashing gongs and beating drums of the orchestra.

Baigujing turned toward me, and I recognized her as Deng Aili, the performer from the photograph on the shrine wall. Her eyes were wide and desperate; I couldn't tear my gaze away. I blinked, and I was staring at my own face, gaping up from the aisle like a pop-eyed goldfish. I stumbled with the weight of something heavy atop my head. The audience jeered, filling me with incandescent rage—how *dare* they—and I snarled at them, screaming, with a throaty, wild, impossible pitch. Everyone froze. Sun Wukong was caught mid-flip; he hung upside-down, suspended in the air. Greedily, I grabbed his face, turning it to whisper into his ear. *"Your turn."* Then I dug my nails into his cheek and scratched, the points sharp as blades, watching with pleasure as lines of liquid red formed in their wake, dripping down his forehead, into his hair. His eyes bulged and strained, but still, he could not move anything else. I licked blood from his eyeball; it tasted sweet as honey.

Slowly, gently, I ran my nails across Sun Wukong's throat,

watching with delight as his tender skin split apart.

Deep in my core, an ancient thing unloosed itself. It bubbled up in my lungs and throat, erupting as a cackle that echoed throughout the auditorium. My mind pulled apart, overwhelmed by conflicting images and sounds. I was onstage, yet simultaneously seated in the audience, unable to move, mouth agape as I watched blood drip from the Monkey King's lacerated neck. The unhinged, crowing laughter was mine, and it was hers, powerful enough to reverberate through every bone in my frozen body.

Aili and I were both one and separate, her joy layered over my horror.

Cymbals clashed, releasing everyone from their prison, and Sun Wukong wasn't dead. His mask and clothes were stained red, but he was alive, and when he lunged this time, there was no performance in it. He was all teeth and uncontrolled anger and the kind of outraged ferocity that only comes from a man denied something he believes is *his*. My thrill turned to fear as he wrapped his hands around my throat, lifted me in the air, and squeezed. I tried to scream, but he had stolen my voice, and I watched as his face morphed into a familiar one, into the man who had haunted my nightmares for ten long years, the last man I saw before—

With a growl, he flung me off the stage. My head hit the floor. The Opera House shook, as if struck by an earthquake, and then everything went black.

CHAPTER 5

My head exploded with pain as my ears filled with a loud, rhythmic pounding. I cried out, curling up and clutching my temple, unsure where I was or how I'd gotten here.

Eventually, the headache subsided, though my cheek still throbbed something fierce. I lay on my back for several minutes until I caught my breath. It was dark and cold, and the moon was a sliver, seeping in through familiar windows above.

Tears streamed down my face. When I wiped them away, I felt scratch marks, and my palms came back slick red. Sun Wukong's ugly leer flashed through my mind, accompanied by the echo of Deng Aili's laughter. I felt suddenly exposed. Even with my eyes starting to adjust, it was hard to be sure I was alone in the auditorium.

As I pushed to my feet, something pressed into the crown of my head, weighing it down. I reached up to feel the memory of a headdress. But there was nothing there, and the sensation of heaviness vanished. With tentative fingers, I checked my face again.

This time, the skin was smooth, uncut. What the hell had happened and where had the blood come from?

I had never sleepwalked before then, nor was I accustomed to dreams that vivid. Confusion and frustration flowed through me in waves. My bare feet tingled where they were pressed against the theater floor. The Opera House felt alive, like I could sense every bone and sinew of the centuries-old building.

With shaky steps, I traced the path back to my room. This time, the corridor looked plain, cast in pale yellow by modern lightbulbs. Of course. They would never risk an open fire hazard in an old wooden building. How had I ever imagined these narrow passageways resembling a wide, candle-lit cavern?

In the bathroom I'd scrubbed earlier that day, I splashed my face, watching pink water swirl down the drain. A careful inspection in the mirror yielded no answers; the origin of my bloody cheek remained a mystery. When the water ran clear again, I could almost believe it had all been my imagination.

On my way back, I noticed a light shining through the paper screen door of one of the rooms. Someone else was up.

The hall was just bright enough to illuminate a brush-painted sign.

克琳
Kristy

She'd said I could come find her anytime for an impromptu singing lesson.

I shook my head, trying to hammer some sense into my tired mind. Obviously, Kristy hadn't meant for me to bother her at this hour. I didn't need a reputation as the creepy girl who harassed performers at night. I knew I should return to my room.

But her light was on, so she was probably awake. And right then, the thought of returning to my dark, lonely room felt unbearable.

Torn, I glanced down the hall, willing myself to continue. It looked narrower than I recalled, the pathway ahead barely lit. Several lightbulbs flickered as if on the verge of death. I couldn't shake the feeling that if I continued down that path, a vicious, formless thing would snatch me from the shadows and pull me into the walls; that the Opera House would swallow me whole.

Shivering, I knocked. When no one answered, I slid open the door. Warmth radiated from inside, pleasant as the tickle of a cozy fire. "Kristy?" I called softly. No reply.

Kristy's room made mine look like a closet. She had enough space for an entryway console, which held a vase of blooming flowers and several framed accolades. Her furniture set was lacquered black and ornate, like it had been plucked out of an ancient Chinese lithograph. On the wall across from her bed hung a floor-length mirror, frame carved with dragons, phoenixes, and bats. It drew me forward, and I touched my reflection, the glow of the hallway light casting eerie shadows on my face.

I imagined Kristy standing here, singing softly.

Behind my mirror self, something shone bright. I turned to see a laptop, open and unlocked. She must have been here recently; it was odd we hadn't crossed paths in the hallway. My eyes landed on the screen, and shock ran through me as I recognized the image on the open browser. The same picture I'd seen in the shrine.

Deng Aili, the opera singer in white.

Dashing forward, I pressed a key before the computer could lock me out. The article accompanying the photo was in Chinese, of course. I couldn't read it. Within me, frustration boiled as I noticed more tabs featuring various articles, all in Chinese.

With the aid of a translation site, I tried to piece together the contents of the article, slogging through nonsensical sentences. Between my still-sluggish brain and racing heart, focus felt impossible. I was half convinced I'd be caught snooping at any moment.

What would happen to Mom and me if I got us kicked out? Did we have anywhere left to go?

After several painful minutes of garbled reading, I thought of an easier way. I logged into my email; not an easy task in Chinese, but I'd memorized the motions during the months Mom and I lived in our previous apartment, when we'd had to borrow all our electronics from her controlling ex. I drafted a new message, copied the links to each article, and sent them to Yi along with a quick note.

My best friend had lived in Shanghai until she was ten. After moving to the United States, her parents sent her to supplementary Chinese school. She'd be able to translate.

Heart still pounding, I signed out of my account and returned the screen to the article featuring Deng Aili's photo. Unease filled me as I imagined Kristy returning to find someone she barely knew sitting at her desk, suspicion and anger growing as she saw my guilt-ridden face.

As I was about to leave, my eyes caught on a sliver of wrongness on one side of the mirror. I knew I should ignore it—every moment here was a risk—but I couldn't help myself. I peered closer, running my fingers down the side. There was a slight gap. With my breath held, I listened for footsteps from the hallway.

Silence.

I pulled, and the mirror slid open to reveal a dark corridor.

Curiosity propelled me forward. I stepped into the shadows, each tread a whisper against the stone passageway.

In a theater with three hundred years of history, secret corridors might have had any number of uses. I imagined servants scurrying quietly throughout the building or paramours using tunnels to slip into one another's rooms after dark. Was that where Kristy had gone? Siquan mentioned something about Kristy's rich K-pop fiancé, and Kristy had referred to him as Joon-Ho. That couldn't be the same Joon-Ho that Yi sometimes mentioned when she swooned over her favorite bands, could it?

I tried to imagine Kristy stashing away a world-famous K-pop star in one of the tiny, ancient Opera House rooms, and I burst into giggles. If Joon-Ho was around there somewhere, I'd have to get his autograph for Yi.

The passageway smelled damp. I pressed my sleeve over my face, hoping I wasn't breathing in toxic mold.

Somewhere up ahead, I caught a glimpse of unsteady light. A spider jumped on my shoulder, and I squeaked, nearly squishing it in my haste to brush it off me. My heartbeat quickened as I imagined what else might lie in wait. I swallowed down my fear, forcing myself to take another step forward.

A cold hand snatched my arm.

I screamed, but another hand clamped over my mouth.

Panicked, I bit my kidnapper's fingers. They cursed, the sound loud in my ear. I twisted to face my attacker, who grunted as I kneed them in the stomach and shoved them backward. They groaned as they hit the stone floor.

"Megan, stop!"

The voice gave me pause. Something scuttled across my

foot as I took a step back. I screamed again as the critter vanished into the stonework.

"It's *me*!"

My heart was beating hard enough to burst out of my chest. I forced myself to focus, squinting at the figure on the floor, a dark silhouette against the light coming in from Kristy's room. *"Mom?"*

"What the hell, Megan?"

"I..." The words died on my tongue as my mind struggled to make sense of the situation. I had no idea how to explain any of my decisions since leaving the auditorium. Why *had* I done those things?

"That hurt!" Mom sat up. The motion snapped me out of my stupor, and I helped her stand.

"I didn't know it was you."

She rubbed the back of her head, wincing.

"Are you okay?" I whispered.

Instead of responding, Mom dragged me back into Kristy's room by the arm, firmly shutting the mirror behind us. Then she fixed a furious gaze on me. "Megan, what were you thinking? You shouldn't leave your room at night!"

"I didn't mean to! I was sleepwalking or something and woke up in the auditorium."

"What! You've never been a sleepwalker."

"I *know*, Mom."

"Why didn't you come get me?"

"I don't even know where your room is!" I was practically shouting. What did she expect from me?

"Oh." Dark circles lined Mom's eyes. She glanced around. "We can't stay here. Come on."

"Wait! Why is there a passage back there?"

"Let's go. *Now*, Megan." Her voice was ragged as she pulled me out of the room, looking around the hallway before shutting the door firmly. I glanced over to see just how much trouble I was in, and I was surprised to see her hand trembling. I'd never seen her look this afraid; not even when we'd lived with monsters.

"My room is the other way. And you're hurting me."

Mom loosened her grip. "I'm showing you where my room is."

The silence between us was unusually tense. I felt an urge to fill it, to smooth things over the way she always expected me to. The story sat at the tip of my tongue—all the details of my strange, waking nightmare, my inexplicable bloody cheek, the articles on Kristy's laptop. But telling her would only worry her more, adding pressure when she seemed frail already. I bit back my words.

As we passed one of the hallway lights, I noticed Mom wasn't wearing makeup. Faded purple patches blotched her cheek in uneven patterns. She'd be mortified if anyone caught her like that. She must have been sleeping before she'd run out to fetch me.

Mom's room looked similar to mine. I sat on her bed, shifting uncomfortably as she looked me over. I couldn't tell what she sought, but I hoped I'd been thorough in washing off the blood.

When she started fussing with my hair, I couldn't stand it anymore. It was too much like all the times she tried to pretty me up and talk me into going to parties with the friends she seemed convinced I could make—even though she moved us constantly. Or the times she'd unsubtly tried to set me up with random boys whose fathers she knew. She'd always wanted me to be just like her.

I pushed her hand away. "I still don't get it. How did you find me?"

Mom looked annoyed. "I had insomnia, so I went to your room, but you weren't there. There was only one room with a light on, so I went in and checked. Megan, you can't just snoop around."

"I didn't mean to snoop! I was confused, and I thought you were asleep already, and Kristy is the only other person here that I know. I didn't want to be alone."

Mom sighed, wrinkle lines crinkling her eyelids. "I'm sorry. I should have shown you where my room was immediately."

"It's fine."

She rubbed her temples. "I've had trouble sleeping too. The air here is... strange after so long."

"You've been here before?"

She blinked. "You know I grew up in Beijing. I watched a few performances here when I was young."

"Right." I studied Mom, feeling like there was more she wasn't saying. The bags beneath her eyes were dark and puffy. I felt bad for scaring her so badly. And for shoving her.

Mom gave me a long hug. "Wei said he'll get us tickets to see the show next week. We're gonna have fun here, you'll see." I wondered which of us she was trying to convince.

"Okay." I stood to leave, but she insisted I lie down on her bed. I curled up and she sat beside me, petting my hair the way she used to when I was a little girl.

She seemed exhausted, so I wasn't surprised when she passed out, her snores filling the room. I closed my eyes and tried to rest. But every time I began to drift off, images flashed through my mind—Sun Wukong's neck split open, my own wide-eyed terror as I stood rigid in the audience—and I opened my eyes again, heart pounding. At last, I gave up and tiptoed out.

Back in my room, I was reluctant to try sleeping again, afraid I'd fall into another nightmare. The book sat on my nightstand, where I'd left it earlier in the evening. Settling into bed, I picked it up and continued reading.

At last, Baigujing had recouped enough strength for a final attempt. This time, she grew a long, wispy beard, wrinkled her skin, and twisted her back until she resembled an elderly man. With meditation beads in one hand and sutras in the other, she approached Tang Sanzang and his disciples. Baigujing was delighted to see that Sun Wukong was not with the group, but she kept her smile hidden as she deliberately stumbled into the monk's path.

"Gōnggong, are you well?" Tang Sanzang held the old man's shoulders to steady him. "We did not mean to block your path."

"You should watch where you step," the old man scolded, snatching up the fallen meditation beads. "I have lost so much already. Oh, you must protect me! A village boy told me he saw the Monkey King himself kill my wife! I did not want to believe him, and yet you, Sun Wukong's sworn master, are here. And now I'm left to wonder if the wretched monkey also killed my only daughter. He has gone back to his wicked ways! I do not know what my family has done to gain his wrath, but you must save me!"

"I apologize for the unforgivable sins my disciple has committed. He is haring off in search of a demon he insists is out there, but I am afraid you are quite right. He must be having some sort of delusion. We will certainly..."

Tang Sanzang was cut off by Sun Wukong's return. As soon as the Monkey King saw the old man, he lunged, staff held above his head. Baigujing shrank back as Tang Sanzang spoke the secret words taught to him by the bodhisattva Guanyin.

Sun Wukong dropped his staff and began screaming as spiders of pain crawled through his head, lighting his nerves on fire. His staff fell on the old man, its power injuring him. The old man took the opportunity to escape, hobbling away while the furious monk berated his errant disciple.

"You are irredeemable! I hereby banish you from our company. Do not show your face again."

The Monkey King could only whimper in response, sharp pain still stabbing throughout his head.

Heart heavy, Tang Sanzang and his remaining two disciples continued climbing the Mountain of Flowers and Fruit.

From a safe distance, Baigujing watched, pleased to see that her prey was headed straight for her cave.

CHAPTER 6

I woke with the taste of monk's flesh on my tongue. A sweet, fleeting memory that made me want to lay my head back down on the pillow for the chance it would return.

I found a tube of toothpaste in my stash, squeezed a drop directly onto my tongue, and swirled it around, coating my mouth with mint. The taste was strong enough to make me gag, but at least it chased away the craving.

I swallowed, savoring the burn of mint, and got dressed.

The thought of breakfast turned my stomach, so I skipped the restaurant, choosing to wander the building instead.

In the shrine, I stared into Deng Aili's eyes. My strange, sleepwalking dream from the night before had felt so vivid, so real. The muscles in my back still ached, as if I'd actually danced the opera. And I could still see Sun Wukong's twisted expression in that moment right before he threw me off the stage.

I forced the images away and headed for the auditorium.

While I wasn't eager to deal with Siquan and the rest of the performers, something drew me there. This time, I'd be careful to stay hidden.

The signs were all in Chinese, so I made my best guess based on location. There was a dingy red door with a discolored handle at the back of the building that looked promising. It took three tries, the last of which left a streak of rusty orange on my palm, before the door swung open. Flakes of red paint fell as I stepped into a dark room.

I was surrounded by heads.

My eyes landed on a giant, gray-pink face, and I leapt back, heart pounding. I couldn't make myself look away; its features were oddly proportioned and hyper-realistic. Its prominent snout, huge ears, and wrinkly forehead made its empty, beady black eyes look unusually small. Tufts of fuzzy white hair sprouted along its chin, cheeks, and eyebrows. Beside it was another oversized head covered in fish scales. Its puckered lips moved yet formed no sound.

Without meaning to, I'd backed up against the door. Air suddenly blasted through the vent, and I jumped, ready to scramble back into the hall... until my eyes landed on a familiar shade of tawny fur. Sun Wukong.

Of course; this must be the costume room. A helpless giggle escaped my mouth. This place was fucking with my sense of reality. I forced myself to walk back up to the masks, to peer into the hollow eye sockets of Zhu Bajie and Sha Wujing. To *get a grip*.

Behind them, Tang Sanzang's crown sat atop a faceless mannequin. I reached out, running my fingers along the intricate beadwork. Down one of the long strips of white silk meant to cover his ears. My fingertip slipped, brushing the mannequin's cheek. It was warm and soft, like skin.

My mouth watered.

I pulled my hand back and gulped down my saliva, forcing myself to step away.

With sudden clarity, I realized how bad an idea it was for me to be there. The masks looked expensive, precious. This place had to be forbidden to outsiders.

Why had the door been unlocked?

The skin on the back of my neck prickled; I felt like a rabbit sensing a nearby predator. I surveyed the room, gaze sweeping past a rack full of heavy-looking costumes, a table piled high with palettes of makeup, and shelves of props.

A huge headdress, just like the one I'd worn in my dream the night before, sat alone in one corner. Like the masks and crown, it was mounted on a gray mannequin. But this one was carved with distinctive features—and it looked old. Ancient. Its cheek was sunken in, and part of it had torn off. I could've sworn its lips were curved into a smile.

I lifted Baigujing's headdress off the mannequin and tried it on. It was so heavy I had to focus to keep my head stable. I felt around for buttons or clips—something to keep it secure—but couldn't find any. Figuring it must attach through hair combs or something, I began pulling it off to take a closer look.

It was stuck.

My chest grew tight, my breathing strained. I pulled harder, but the headdress wouldn't budge. My scalp grew tender as I tried again and again to pry it off. I knew I should stop, that I was damaging my hair—Mom's favorite feature of mine—but panic fueled me. My eyes filled with tears.

There was a noise behind me. Still clutching the headdress, I turned to see the door handle jiggling.

Shit. There was nowhere to hide.

The door opened. Kristy's eyebrows lifted as she registered me standing there in Baigujing's headdress. My cheeks reddened. It seemed I was destined to find myself in humiliating circumstances every time we met. If she'd found out about my snooping through her room, it would be even worse.

I searched her face for signs of suspicion. Maybe I'd left evidence behind. Maybe someone had seen me and Mom leave Kristy's room. Maybe Kristy was a computer whiz with a tracking program that told her if someone used her laptop. Maybe...

"Are you okay?" Kristy seemed genuinely concerned. She didn't sound like she was about to report me to Wei or someone else.

"It won't come off." My voice came out brittle.

She moved toward me. "Tip your head forward." I did as

she said, and she slid her fingers between my scalp and the headdress. The weight lifted, and my head felt free again.

Relief flooded me. "How did you do that?"

"It happens sometimes." Kristy sounded absent, attention on the headdress in her hands. She turned it over, inspecting each surface with a careful eye. She was checking for damage.

Any case I'd felt was gone in an instant. I might've gotten Mom and myself kicked out, after all. "Did I break it?"

Kristy finished her inspection and shook her head. "Nah." She set down the headdress. "What were you doing in here anyway?"

"I, um, was looking for you?" I cleared my throat. "I got lost."

"Oh! Okay... did you need something?"

"Yeah, I mean, I was wondering if your offer was still open. For singing lessons. If you're free." I cursed my own awkwardness, but Kristy just nodded.

"Sure! The troupe's off today, so we can use the theater. Come on."

Kristy took off at a brisk stride. I followed her out of the costume room, through a maze of back doors and tight corners. The backstage area was a lot bigger than I'd expected.

"This is the fastest way?"

Ahead of me, Kristy shrugged. "There's usually a more direct path, but it's blocked by the renovations."

"Oh yeah. I heard something about that."

"The theater always seems to be rotting somewhere.

Buildings that have lived through as much as Huihuang has need care." Kristy's voice was low and distant. It was the same tone she'd used to caution me yesterday.

"What do you mean?" My mind raced through the articles I'd copied from her computer. I needed to find a way to check in with Yi to see if she'd learned anything.

Kristy didn't answer. I wasn't sure if she'd missed my question or her silence was intentional. Before I had the chance to ask again, she opened a side door, and we entered the stage.

It felt wrong being in there; just us two in a space meant to be shared by thousands. I was reminded of the time Mom and I did a cross-country road trip, stopping at what her ex called "liminal spaces" across America.

He had been obsessed with them, always going on about how they were the souls of dying places. It was originally a plan for all three of us, but a week before the trip, he accused her of cheating on him. They broke up, and Mom and I hopped in her beat-up Subaru and left for an impromptu tour. A combination of revenge, and proof we didn't need him. Mom tried to make it seem fun and exciting, but my nine-year-old self was more creeped out than anything by the deserted malls, old train stations, weird hotels with endless-seeming hallways, and abandoned water parks we visited.

Surrounded by all those empty seats in the grand, silent theater, I felt like a child again.

Gradually, a new sensation rose. I couldn't explain, but I

felt certain someone was watching me and Kristy. I shivered, scanning the room for hidden viewers, and found none. This should've been reassuring; instead, my unease deepened.

Though I was nervous at first, I took my cue from Kristy. She stood onstage with a confidence I wished I had, singing to the vacant room with all her heart. Her voice was strong and beautiful, possibly even lovelier than it had been the previous day. No one could improve that quickly, could they? For a moment, I forgot where we were. Why we were here. I could've lain down there and died happy, listening.

She finished her song and turned to smile, eyes bright. "Your turn!"

"I thought you were giving me lessons."

"Yeah, but it'll help me to hear you sing. That way, I can see where your strengths lie so I can gauge what we should focus on."

My voice wavered at first, and I stopped, ready to call it a day. But Kristy was kind and encouraging. She sang a Chinese song even I recognized—a kids' song Mom used to sing to me—exaggerating the highs and lows. When she was done, she dropped into a dramatic bow, refusing to stand back up until I'd stepped into center stage. I couldn't help but laugh, begrudgingly walking to the spot she'd pointed at. She joined me and started singing scales. Before I knew it, I was singing along with her, my voice growing louder and stronger.

It was beautiful, singing to the theater.

∽

After Kristy left to meet up with her boyfriend—yes, she told me, he was *that* Joon-Ho—I stood onstage alone, my throat still full of song. I sipped from the water bottle she'd left me, then I stood tall. I was in the same spot I'd been in the previous night, during my waking dream. With each breath I took, I felt the theater come alive, like we were one. Like it had been deep in slumber, and it was finally awakening. If places could hold power, this one was ripe with it.

I opened my mouth, notes at the tip of my tongue.

Instead of the exercises Kristy taught me, it was Eponine's "On My Own" that spilled out. I closed my eyes as I sang, letting each verse sweep me away to a past long gone. To the days when Mom and I lived with Dad. The three of us crowded into a tiny second-story apartment, singing show tunes together while the downstairs neighbor yelled at us to shut up. Dad laughing and kissing Mom. The two of them looking at me with matching grins, whispering. *Should we sing louder?*

My cheeks grew wet. To my teenaged self, my standing there singing to an empty stage was the closest I'd ever get to the future Dad promised we'd have. The one where we stayed a family. Where Dad worked a job fancy enough to pay for my singing lessons and Mom shuttled me to practice every day after school for years and years. Where I grew up and moved to New York City.

Dad always made me promise I'd save him and Mom front-row seats when I made it big as a Broadway star.

I sang until my face was drenched. Until my throat was dry. Until there was nothing left but broken promises and dreams that died before they had the chance to live.

CHAPTER 7

On an afternoon a few days later, I'd just finished scrubbing the public bathrooms yet again—my least favorite job, for obvious reasons. After stashing away the cart and punching out, I headed to the teahouse for a snack.

In the hallway, the sound of arguing caught my attention from one of the storage rooms up ahead. Nearing, I recognized Kristy's voice through the closed door. She was quarreling with someone in Mandarin; I concentrated hard, doing my best to piece together their words.

Kristy thought something was a waste of time, and someone argued back that it was important. It—whatever that was—would draw interest. And then something else I didn't understand.

Was that Wei? I tensed, listening for other voices, but no one else chimed in. Kristy had said she didn't like Wei, and as far as I could tell, she might be alone with him now. I didn't know what was going on, but it didn't feel right to leave without checking to make sure everything was okay.

I opened the door without knocking.

Wei was mid-sentence. At the sound of creaking hinges, he cut off abruptly. Both he and Kristy looked at me, surprised.

"Oh, hi! What's going on?" I asked. Immediately, I felt foolish. Kristy was older than me. She didn't need me to rescue her.

"This jerk wants the troupe to spend our next day off doing a photoshoot for some magazine. He thinks it'll make him look impressive to his rich friends." Kristy was seething.

"That's not true!" Wei turned to me with that fake, cordial smile he'd worn when we'd first met. "Of course, that's not why. I only want the show to do well. To keep Chinese opera alive. This will bring much-needed publicity!"

"Yeah, publicity is great, but you can't keep pulling stunts like this without advance notice! There was that last-minute meet and greet when your friend's son was in town, and the TV segment you conveniently forgot to tell us about until the day of. I don't care if this magazine had an unexpected opening thanks to some cancellation or whatever. We've been rehearsing and performing nearly every day. We deserve a break." Kristy glared at him.

Wei's face colored, and I could see the annoyance he was trying to keep hidden. He took a deep breath, but I took that moment to speak first. "My mom says rest is necessary for artists to thrive. Rested performers will put on a better show, and a spectacular performance is the best publicity." The whole *rest is necessary* thing was actually based on something Yi had said—but I knew Wei wouldn't care unless I invoked Mom.

Wei worried his lip as he eyed me. I felt like we were in a game of chicken. He was still in the *play nice* stage of wooing Mom. He obviously wanted me to like him. Maybe he thought he and Mom would get married and I'd be his new stepdaughter or something. Gross.

There were so few times where I had any kind of upper hand. I felt a rush at the thought of using what little I had to help out someone who had shown me kindness.

Finally, Wei nodded, offering me another weak smile. "You're right, of course." He turned to Kristy. "I will call them back now and tell them we need more notice to schedule an appropriate date."

"Fine," Kristy said.

Wei left the room. Once his footsteps had receded, Kristy sat on the floor, sighing as she leaned against the wall. I sat down beside her.

"I don't know why I let him get to me. I know I'm supposed to be professional, that I should just tell him no without all the insults. It's just... people like him are always taking, always trying to get more out of us artists. They don't care if they burn us out as long as they get as much money as they can, first. And Wei, especially, drives me up the wall. He shows us off to his little friends with such pride, as if *he* was the one busting his ass onstage four nights a week." She made a frustrated sound and punched the wall lightly.

At her words, happiness bubbled up inside me, and I immediately felt guilty. She had taken me into her confidence, and a horrible side of me was glad to bear witness to these moments of impulse and frustration. I found relief in Kristy's imperfection. It might be hard for you to believe, but back then, I could scarcely imagine what it was like to live a life like hers.

She sighed again. "It's always like this, the commodification of art. And, truth is, a magazine feature probably *is* good for the troupe. But hell, I'm tired. We're all tired."

I thought of Kristy's room, empty in the middle of the night. "You work hard."

"Yeah." She smiled at me. "I'm glad you got him to back down. How did you do that?"

"I know his type."

Kristy frowned, and I worried I'd said too much. But all she said was, "Thank you."

"It's nothing."

"Hey, I was going to go shopping today. Joon-Ho's sister is throwing a dinner party next week, and I need a new dress. Want to come with?"

I swallowed hard. My shift was done, and I desperately wanted to say yes, but shopping made me nervous. It would be near impossible to hide that I was broke.

Kristy noticed my hesitation. "It'll be fun. Have you been to Wángfǔjǐng? There's a ton of stores there, plus a whole street dedicated to snack stands! We can browse a few shops and then grab dinner."

"I, um... don't have money of my own." I hoped she wouldn't read between the lines and realize Mom didn't have money either. Mom hated people knowing.

Kristy's eyes widened as understanding dawned. "Oh, don't worry about that! It's my treat."

"I can't..."

"Consider it compensation for getting me out of that situation with Wei. Seriously, I should hire you as my manager. You call tell off all the assholes. Come on, let's go! It's boring shopping alone, and I love my troupe, but we see each other all the fucking time. I'm sick of them."

I wondered if she was just saying that to make me feel better. But a snack street *did* sound cool. And didn't I deserve some fun after scrubbing all those toilets?

⁓

Kristy, of course, looked stunning in everything. I had never really been into clothing; it was hard to be when you were broke. My wardrobe was a hodgepodge of things Mom had picked out for me from the thrift store, hand-me-downs from Mom or Yi or various others, and the occasional new item from when Mom happened to have a wealthy boyfriend. I had no idea what to do when faced with so many options, nor did I know what would flatter my shape and complexion.

Kristy, on the other hand, had an expert eye. After I'd picked out a few ill-fitting garments to try on, she sized me up and collected several pieces I would never have thought to try. They fit me beautifully. I marveled in the mirror, heart breaking a little, knowing I couldn't afford any of it.

For the dinner party, Kristy chose a gorgeous navy dress. When she went to check out, she quietly added a soft white sleeveless top I'd fallen in love with. I tried to protest, but she said it was the least she could do when she'd dragged me out for the evening.

That first time we'd met, Kristy had rescued me from Siquan and his drunken rage. She'd invited me to tea, and she hadn't told anyone when she'd found me snooping in the room full of masks. She'd promised me singing lessons, then actually followed through. She was like a glamorous older sister, protective and kind and immensely talented. She was the kind of jiějie I would've wanted to be, if I'd had the chance.

If only.

I'd thought the main shopping street was overwhelming—massive buildings with signage taller than me, giant television screens playing looped ads, and an abundance of pedestrians loaded up with shopping bags. Still, I didn't start feeling claustrophobic until I followed Kristy through a grand, colorful archway leading to a narrower road.

There, countless vendors lined both sides of the street, hawking their wares from carts that sat beneath tiled roof awnings. The snack street was a deluge of sounds, smells, and colors, and there were people everywhere. I was not yet used to the cultural differences in acceptable personal space, and for a moment, it was too much. But Kristy was already weaving her way through the crowd. I took a deep breath and followed.

As Kristy and I ordered little platters of dumplings, steamed rice cakes, sugar-coated haws, jiānbǐng, and yogurt-in-a-jar to share, I found myself wishing I could cruise through life the way she did. That I didn't have to think, always, about how much everything cost or how to keep Mom's latest boyfriend appeased.

We returned home late that evening, and Kristy bade me goodnight. I tucked away my new shirt, knowing that if Mom saw, she'd be upset that I'd let Kristy buy it for me. I would save it for the inevitable next time we moved, a souvenir to remind me of someone kind I'd met once upon a time, when I'd lived in an opera house.

CHAPTER 8

Between the fifteen-hour time difference, Yi's schedule, and my lack of a computer, it was several days before she and I were finally able to chat. Mom had been afraid to bring any of our electronics when we'd fled, paranoid they might be bugged by her ex. I'd had to eat my pride and ask Wei to lend me a laptop.

"I looked at the articles," Yi said.

"I knew I could count on you." I sipped lychee boba, gazing out onto the Opera House's private garden from my seat on the teahouse patio. Koi swam in a nearby pond, scales shimmering with reflected sunlight. Between the tall white walls, soft background music, and lush summer greenery, it felt like a tiny oasis.

"Yep, I'm awesome."

I grinned. God, I missed Yi. She was the only friend I'd kept through all the moves. When we'd met in school six years earlier, everyone had lumped us together—two Chinese girls new to super-white Portland, Oregon. No matter that Yi had been from Shanghai, and I'd most recently come from Stockton. I hadn't minded. There'd finally been someone who looked more lost than I did. Mom and I had moved the next year, but Yi kept in touch. We were both thrilled when I'd returned to Portland after a few years away. Portland was home because it was where Yi was.

I wished fervently that Mom and I had stayed there.

"So, what'd you learn?" I asked.

"Most of the articles were about a Chinese opera star from a few decades ago. Deng Aili. Have you heard of her?"

"There's a picture of her at the Opera House. I'm guessing she performed here?"

"Yeah, in the earlier ones, she was described as this young, rising star. Then traditional opera got banned for ten years during the Cultural Revolution. After the ban was lifted and the theaters reopened, she starred in the reopening show at Huihuang—one of the famous operas that depicted a portion of Xīyóujì. I forget if you know it."

Journey to the West, right?"

"Yeah, that one. So, get this. The theater company went *bold*. They picked it *specifically* because the villain in it came to represent Jiāng Qīng—the actress who became Máo Zédōng's fourth wife. As one of the articles put it, she tricked everyone by offering smiles and greetings from the Chairman when in reality, she was a destroyer."

A chill ran down my spine. "Was the show *Sūn Wùkōng Sān Dǎ Báigǔjīng?*"

"Yeah, that's the one! How did you know?"

"That's the opera they're showing here right now."

"Really? Have you seen it yet? I bet the costumes are amazing." I could practically hear Yi drooling over the visuals. She was one of those effortlessly creative types who sewed her own clothing and styled absolutely everything, including the composition of her plate at mealtimes. The pop-up memory scrapbook she'd given me before I'd left Portland was one of the few things I'd packed when Mom and I had fled our last apartment.

"I haven't, but Mom and I have tickets for tomorrow."

"Oh my god, can you *please* film some of it for me? It's probably illegal or something, but you owe me for all this research."

"No phone, remember?"

Yi's expression morphed into pity. "Right, of course."

My face grew hot; I wished the ground would open up and swallow me whole. "I saw a book about Chinese opera costumes in the gift shop here. I'll bring it back for you." I made a mental note to steal the book for her later. Yi gave me a tight smile—we both knew I couldn't afford it. "But you still haven't told me what you learned about Deng Aili."

Yi's eyes lit up. "Right! So, I guess the show started gaining a reputation until all the critics wanted to watch.

The way everyone describes Aili's performance in the role of Baigujing is weirdly reverent. You'd think she invented music, they loved her *that* much. It's almost creepy."

I thought of Kristy's voice, strong and beautiful, filling the auditorium. "Maybe because of the opera ban? Plus, I can't imagine the Cultural Revolution was a great time. Being able to see a show again after a decade of *that* must have felt like magic."

"From the way they go on, it might as well have been. And there's more. Are you ready for the lurid details?" Yi licked her lips.

"Always."

"Midway through the last show of the year, the actor playing Sun Wukong attacked Aili with a real blade. She ran off the stage all bloody and screaming. He went after her and... they never found her again. The only thing they found was her severed tongue. At least, they assumed it was hers."

"Holy shit, Yi! Are you serious?" I swallowed hard, thinking of Sun Wukong's face twisted in hate as he wrapped his hands around my neck. I bit my lip, trying to mask my reaction. The last thing I needed was for Yi to start worrying that I was hallucinating.

"If these articles are real, then... yeah."

"Oh my god."

"Yep." Yi slurped her smoothie. Nothing fazed her.

"Did they catch the attacker?"

"Here's the clincher. They found the actor playing Sun Wukong knocked out in a closet. It must have happened sometime between the scenes. Aili's murderer managed to suit up and get back onstage as Sun Wukong. Or maybe he was in a costume the entire time, waiting to jump the actor. The only person who saw him up close would have been Aili. They never found out who did it."

"Ugh." Secretly, I hoped it wasn't a recent event. If it was, the murderer could still be alive. I tried to recall when the Cultural Revolution had happened, but it was a lost cause. My patchwork American education hadn't taught me even the basics of Chinese history. "How long ago was this?"

"1977."

Exactly four decades earlier. Four, the unluckiest number according to Chinese superstition. I shivered, thinking of some poor sap finding Aili's tongue. It had probably been a cleaner, like me. "Damn, Yi. Anything else interesting in the articles?"

"Yeah! Some were about other performers—a dancer, a musician, and a singer—whose fame grew for a few years. All of them disappeared pretty young. I couldn't find a connection until I read the comments on an article about the thirtieth anniversary of Aili's death. Some anonymous poster thinks all three performed at Huihuang near the start of their careers."

"As in... they think the disappearances are related or something?"

"It *is* a little weird that they each disappeared a decade apart. In '87, '97, and '07."

I swallowed. "Didn't anyone look into it? What if Aili's attacker is some serial killer who goes after famous musicians every decade or something?"

Yi shrugged. "There are never any bodies, so people figured they either pissed off the government and disappeared... or they left of their own volition for whatever reason. I sent you an email with more info."

"You're the best."

"I know." Yi took another slurp of smoothie. "Anyway, gotta run. You're lucky your mom never made you go to Chinese school. Bye, Megs."

"See ya."

Yi's comment about Chinese school was part of our usual ribbing, and it shouldn't have stung. One benefit to being poor was not having to attend supplementary Chinese school on evenings and weekends the way Yi had, all her life. In the US, it was a way she didn't belong, and I was glad not to be singled out further.

But there, in the capital of China, I felt the ache of everything I'd never learned.

My thoughts turned to Kristy, and the things we'd talked about on our shopping trip. Though she'd been born in Canada and lived there for years, no one questioned her authenticity. No matter where she was or what she was doing,

Kristy seemed to move with effortless ease; like she'd been born to fill whichever role she was playing at the moment.

I had an hour left before my shift started, so I browsed through what Yi had sent, smiling when I saw her research organized into sections with bolded headings. She'd included commentary along with various memes that made me laugh aloud. The sound drew patrons' stares, but I didn't care.

With help from Yi's notes and various translation sites, I took a more in-depth look at the articles.

> Violinist Chén Guóliàng disappeared in 1997, following a successful career. Friends in Vancouver, where Chen lived for eight years, reported strange behavior prior to his disappearance, including a growing obsession with returning to Beijing. "When asked why, he mumbled about impossible things. We were worried about him," an anonymous source said. One month after moving his family, Chen disappeared, leaving behind his seven-year-old daughter.

I read several more articles, ending on one written about Huihuang Opera House in 1997, accompanied by a photo. A group of performers posed together in front of the building, huddled close. They looked happy, most holding up a victory sign with their fingers. I couldn't help smiling as I scanned their faces... until I saw a girl off to the right. She was playfully slapping at the guy behind her, who was giving her bunny ears. Even though she was young in the photos, I recognized her.

Mom.

I kept looking at the photo like it would change, but no matter how hard I stared, it was still Mom smiling up at her friend; a sweet, carefree look I'd rarely seen.

Jealousy coursed through me, followed by annoyance. She'd mentioned watching performances at the theater, but being *in them* was different. How could she not tell me?

I ran through everything Mom had said over the previous few days. Deep down, I'd known she was hiding something from me, but I'd tried to give her the benefit of the doubt. Like I always did.

I wondered again how she'd known about the passageway behind Kristy's mirror. Had she really stumbled across it while looking for me, like she'd claimed? At the time, I'd been too tired and worried about getting in deeper trouble. And then, between hanging out with Kristy and starting work, I'd forgotten about it.

Looking back, Mom's story seemed far-fetched.

I arranged two of the browser windows so that Deng Aili's photo sat next to the photo of Mom at Huihuang Opera House. I stared at them, mentally replaying the events of the night I'd sleepwalked. I focused extra hard on everything that had happened after I'd seen Kristy's light on. Tried to remember exactly what Mom had said after she'd pulled me out of the weird tunnel and made excuses for why she'd been there.

When the realization hit, I couldn't believe I hadn't seen it sooner. That feeling when I'd seen Deng Aili's photo, first in the Opera House shrine, then on Kristy's screen. *That's why she'd seemed familiar.*

Mom used to look at it when she'd thought I wasn't watching. More than once, I'd walked in and caught her holding it in her hands, staring, face unreadable.

Mom had a photo of Deng Aili.

CHAPTER 9

Mom was still working when I finished my shift. I was pissed she'd lied, but I knew I needed to be strategic if I wanted any real answers. When it came to deflection, she was the master.

She promised we'd go to dinner after work, so I headed back to my room to wait for her. I sat on my bed and picked up *Journey to the West*. But before I could begin, there was a knock. I slid open the door, figuring Mom must have finished up early.

"Hey, Megan." Wei grinned.

I stepped forward to block the entrance, folding my arms. No way was I letting that creep come into my room.

Wei backed away, holding his hands up. "I just came to bring you something." He pulled something out of his back pocket—ew—and handed it to me.

The cover featured a stylized illustration of Sun Wukong on a cloud, holding Jingu Bang. I couldn't read the title—it was in Chinese—but clearly, this was a copy of *Journey to the West*.

Anger rose within me, sudden and violent. He *knew* I couldn't read this. I was tempted to throw the book at him, but I didn't, for Mom's sake. I'd already made him look bad in front of Kristy. I didn't want to make things worse, in case he was one of those guys who took out his humiliation on women in private.

"I don't need this," I said.

"But it was..."

"No *thanks*."

"I just..."

"Goodbye." I moved to close the door, trying to stay calm.

Wei put up a hand, talking fast. "Wait! Megan, I know we didn't get off to a good start, but it would be nice for your mom if we got along. Jia is a very special woman."

I stared at him, unimpressed. He had no idea how many times I'd heard some variation of this speech.

"Jia tells me you've never been to Chinese opera."

My jaw clenched. Mom knew how much I hated when she told her boyfriends things about me. "So what?"

"It is hard for foreigners to appreciate Chinese opera without being familiar with the story. You are meant to know it already when you watch."

Foreigners. Fuck him.

"The play is part of a famous Chinese classic. It's about a beloved character every child in China knows. The Monkey King—"

"Sun Wukong. Yes, I know."

"I..."

"Thanks." I forced the word out before sliding the door closed. It was a lot less satisfying than slamming the door, but at least I didn't have to see his annoying face anymore. Yet another one of Mom's fucking losers. I never chose them, but I was always stuck with them anyway.

I hurled the book at the corner of the room, feeling a spike of satisfaction when it slammed against the wall and thumped to the ground. Then I lay on the bed and closed my eyes, imagining it was just me and Mom, and we were living somewhere normal. An apartment in the Hawthorne district overlooking a cute coffee shop, across the street from a boutique where Mom worked the register. She'd be good at charming customers into buying prints from local artists. Yi would visit on weekends, using Mom's discount to get one of those weird, Portland-y handcrafted yeti mugs she was obsessed with.

Eventually, the dream grew sour with the taste of things that would never be. I took a deep breath and sat back up, digging around for my copy of the book. Not the one Wei had brought me, and *not* because of what he'd said. I'd been planning to read it anyway. I wanted to know what happened.

As I thumbed through, looking for my spot, I wondered who'd chosen to translate the story from the villain's perspective. It was a departure from pretty much every mythology tale I'd ever read, and I couldn't imagine the original would have centered the White Bone Demon.

Baigujing waited inside the cave, the hunger for monk's flesh so strong her stomach clenched in knots, a constant reminder that her desires had yet to be fulfilled. At last, the most powerful member of the group had been banished, leaving the credulous monk vulnerable. A grin split her face as she set her trap.

Tang Sanzang and his remaining two disciples reached the top of the mountain and entered the cave. Though it had the trappings of a Buddhist temple, the three travelers looked at one another with unease. Something felt wrong. The cavern smelled of sickly-sweet rot, and the thick, soupy air made them gag and cough.

"Master, perhaps we should not be here," Zhu Bajie said.

After the long pilgrimage, Tang Sanzang was reluctant to leave, but he saw the fear in his disciples' eyes and felt the wrongness of the air. He nodded.

At that moment, Baigujing lifted the disguise. The temple disappeared, revealing the cave of the White Bone Demon. All around them, yellowing bones lay in piles. Strips of meat hung from bamboo drying racks. Beneath their feet, many-legged creatures scuttled across the floor, some crawling up their legs.

Zhu Bajie, closest to the cave entrance, slipped out before Baigujing could seal her trap. It was of no concern; she did not care for the flesh of a pig spirit. She had the holy monk now. With haste, Baigujing tied up Tang Sanzang and Sha Wujing. Then she lifted her head and sang, a melody only her fellow demons could hear, calling them to the feast of flesh.

My mouth filled with a taste like pork but stronger, tinged with a hint of bitterness. The flavor grew sweeter, and I started to salivate, licking my lips. An image that felt like a memory flashed through my mind.

My razor-sharp teeth sink into Tang Sanzang's cheek, tearing off a piece. As he screams, the chunk of flesh turns in my mouth. My tongue flicks over the bump of his stubble, already beginning to grow since his morning shave. I savor the chewy fat and the warm, metallic taste of blood dripping down my chin...

I dropped the book, gagging, and ran to the bathroom to throw up.

˞

That evening, Wei joined me and Mom for dinner. Of fucking course. Mom hadn't told me he'd be there, but I wasn't surprised. He didn't mention our chat, so neither did I.

With Wei there, I couldn't ask Mom about anything.

I picked at my food. Wei had ordered Peking duck, going on about how he'd hired the in-house chef specifically for his skill at making this iconic dish. As far as I could tell, it was just another way for him to show off how fabulously rich he was, ordering banquet food for just three people. He bit into the crisp skin and tender meat, chewing with his mouth open. There was a string of duck still stuck in his teeth when he smiled and told me to try it.

Mom gave me a *look*. I glared back at her. Why did I always have to play nice with rotten men who didn't give a shit about either of us? *Please,* she mouthed, eyes wide and pleading.

I sighed and took a bite of duck. It was good. Really good. It reminded me of the taste from earlier—rich and savory, growing sweeter by the moment. My stomach rumbled, and I imagined biting into Tang Sanzang's soft cheek.

I excused myself and ran to the bathroom just in time to vomit again.

My head spun. Where were these images, these false memories, coming from?

By the time I returned to the table, Mom and Wei were squished close together. She fed him a piece of duck meat, giggling. I turned to leave, but Mom spotted me, sat up straight, and waved me back over to join them.

I picked at my plate while Wei whispered something in Mom's ear. I was glad I couldn't understand; from the way she blushed, I assumed I was better off not knowing. When he put his hand on her thigh, I pushed back my chair and stood up.

Mom grabbed my arm. "Stay."

"I have a headache."

"Please. I haven't seen you all day."

I crossed my arms until Wei coughed, inching his chair slightly away from Mom. I couldn't tell if Mom was oblivious or pretending not to notice how uncomfortable I was. Neither option seemed great.

"Dessert will be here soon," Wei said. "Usually, the chefs only make zìláibái and zìláihóng at Zhōngqiū Jié, but I asked them to make them special for us tonight."

Mom smiled up at me. "Growing up here, they were my favorites. I used to hoard them long after Mid-Autumn Fest was over—until they were nearly spoiled—and cry when the last one was gone."

I sat back down. "How come you never told me that before?"

"Because they don't make them anywhere else. Why focus on things we couldn't have?" Mom sighed. "I've missed Beijing."

"Yes, they're very exclusive," Wei said. "Bei-jing mooncakes." He had slowed his speech, enunciating each syllable, as if speaking to a small child. "Named according to their colors. Bái means white and hóng means red."

I took a long sip of water so I wouldn't say something I'd regret. Mom touched Wei's arm gently, and he stopped talking.

As I tried a pine nut and melon seed mooncake—annoyingly tasty—Wei cleared his throat.

"Megan, your mother tells me you enjoy singing."

I shrugged.

"Yes, Megan has a good voice. She had a singing role in

her school's musical." Mom's cheeriness faltered at the end. I glanced over. From the way her gaze immediately flickered away, I knew she was remembering how she'd pulled me out of school before the last show.

"I would be happy to help find you a voice coach," Wei said. "You could have regular lessons."

"No thanks."

"*Megan.*" Mom's voice carried a warning.

"Mom, can I talk to you?"

"Later."

I made an exasperated sound. "You can't just forget about me all of the time!"

Mom turned to Wei. "One moment."

She pulled me out into the hallway. "What is going on with you?"

"Don't you care about me at all? About us?"

Mom's grip on my arm was tight, almost painful, her voice a loud whisper. "Everything I do is for us. Do you understand? *Everything.* I know our lives aren't perfect, but I'm trying. I'm doing my best. Some things are out of my control. But I do love you, and I want you to be happy." She closed her eyes and sucked in a breath, as if she needed to calm herself. As if *I* were the problem.

"I know you're trying. I just... How long are we going to stay here?" I needed her to say she didn't plan to move us into wherever Wei lived. The Opera House might be weird, but it would be better than being trapped in some high-rise with *him*.

Mom sighed. "I don't know. But I will make time for us, okay? We have tomorrow's show, and maybe we can do something this weekend. We can do makeovers and go sightseeing. What do you think?"

"Sure." I knew there was a 50/50 chance she'd forget or cancel.

"And I never, for one moment, forget about you. I keep an eye on you as much as I can, even if you don't know it."

"That's creepy."

Mom rolled her eyes. "Come on. Let's not keep Wei waiting too long."

Back inside, I gritted my teeth and gave my best polite responses to Wei's annoying questions, patently ignoring the many looks passing between him and Mom.

When it was time to pay, Wei swooped in with showy magnanimity, handing the waiter cash while his eyes stayed fixed on Mom. Afterward, Mom and Wei left together, whispering and giggling, and I refused to think about what that meant.

Back in my room, I thumbed through the pages of the costume book I'd stolen for Yi. The paper was thick and full of vivid photographs, each page saturated with the colors of Chinese opera. It was beautiful, but I couldn't fully enjoy it in my mood. Everything felt devoid of meaning.

The photos were interspersed with text—all in Chinese, of course. Longing filled me, accompanied by weariness. Both feelings settled into my bones, ever-present and deep. I ached for this language I wished I could claim. Something permanent; something like a place to belong. As with everything else in my life, my grasp on Chinese was tenuous and unreliable.

I closed the book and tucked it away. It was too early to sleep, but there was nothing to do. I was afraid to pick up Baigujing's story. Afraid reading it would bring back the taste of blood on my tongue, monk's flesh in my teeth.

I decided to head back out, wandering without thinking. Let my feet choose the path; my mind was a swirl of dark thoughts.

Before long, I found myself standing before the door to the auditorium. I opened it and stepped inside. The setting sun filtered through the upper-story windows, breathing rich, tangerine warmth into the room. One last sigh before it sank below the horizon.

I made my way to the stage, the ancient wooden floor creaking with the weight of each footstep. Following what Kristy taught me, I stood in the center, imagined an audience before me, and sang.

Already, my voice felt richer, fuller than before, as if Kristy's lessons had burrowed deep under my skin. I felt like one of the cherry blossoms from the courtyard of the apartment complex Mom and I had fled. A small, inconspicuous thing, any potential to bring beauty to the world still curled up tight within. All I needed was warmth, sun, security for the chance to bloom.

As I sang "Defying Gravity", wishing I had a duet partner, I couldn't stop thinking of Kristy. Rich, beloved, talented, beautiful Kristy who wanted for nothing, who could buy expensive clothing for strangers without a second thought. Who was here by choice. She was like a fairy godmother. Already, I loved her—how could I not? And I resented her.

Night fell; still, I stayed. My throat should have grown parched by then, my voice sore from overuse. Yet I felt nothing but the desire to keep singing, my body no longer fully my own. With each inhale, I felt the power of the Opera House enter my lungs, giving me strength. In the dark it was easier to imagine a full theater, an audience collectively captivated. I could almost see them; twisting shapes and flickering shadows in the darkness. I raised my hands as I sang, and I could have sworn that when I ended the note with a flourish, deep, rumbling applause rang throughout the auditorium.

Power surged through me. Something beyond words or song. Something raw and real.

I felt in control.

A pale, glowing shape emerged from the inky blackness in the back of the theater. I stepped forward, off the stage and up the center aisle, still carrying my song. The floor felt uneven, reminding me of the cobblestoned corridor behind the mirror in Kristy's room. As I neared the door, the vague, luminescent shape coalesced into an emaciated, bone-white hand. It beckoned, inviting me in.

CHAPTER 10

I reached for the hand, but it shimmered and vanished into the darkness. The auditorium's main doors blew wide open, as if hit by a strong gust of wind, and I caught the wisps of an argument. Somewhere down the hall, a low, gruff voice snapped, words terse and angry. Someone else responded, higher in register. Lilting, placating. I didn't recognize the voices, nor could I make out the words—they felt warped and indistinct—but I understood their tones well enough.

I moved toward the sounds, memories racing through my mind. My eight-year-old self, cowering beneath the bed, waiting for it to be over. Again, years later—different man, same entitlement. And then only one month before we ran away to the Opera House. In my mind I saw Mom lying on the floor where *he* had left her, bruises blooming on her face, arm dislocated.

I started running.

It was too soon for Wei to begin growing violent. He was in the wooing stage; he was still enamored of Mom. He wanted to win us over. And maybe he would never become one of the worst ones.

It's not him; it's not Mom. I told myself this over and over, trying to calm my racing heart. But reason couldn't compete with the fear and adrenaline coursing through me, my hyperawareness of every sound in the corridor, the way my entire body had tensed up, making it hard to breathe.

The voices kept moving, changing. It was impossible to tell where they were coming from. The corridor felt endless, twisting and turning in unfamiliar ways. The hallway split into an intersection, and I stopped, feeling a sudden spike of panic. I had no idea where I was. Surely the Opera House could not be this big.

There were no familiar landmarks, only endless, dark screen doors and the eyes of all those ancient carved-wood creatures watching me. Heart pounding, I touched the wall.

"Help me find Mom," I whispered to a serpentine dragon. Desperation left my throat parched. I felt that if I spoke my worries or wishes aloud, they might come true.

The walls shuddered, as if I were in the throat of a great beast as it bellowed laughter. I clung tight, steadying myself.

"*Please.*"

Ahead, a dim light shone, and two voices carried to my ears. Relief swept me forward. I recognized both, and neither was raised in anger.

Through the screen door, shadows cut two silhouettes

from the yellow light. Mom and Wei sat, talking. I wrinkled my nose at his presence, but I was still overwhelmed with gladness that Mom was okay.

"It's a big moment for me. A lot of important people will be there. I want them to meet you." Wei sounded hopeful.

"I would love to be there. Only, I can't leave Megan here by herself."

"She can come with us, of course."

"You said there may be cameras there? Press?"

"Yes!" Wei sounded excited. *"My sister would be happy to go shopping with both of you, I'm sure. Find something suitable."*

"That's kind of her. But I don't think it's a good idea."

In the silence Wei left after Mom's words, I realized they had been speaking in Mandarin. Somehow, I'd understood it as easily as if it were my native tongue.

"Is there a reason you don't want to be seen with me?" Wei's tone sharpened, and my stomach dropped, all my relief vanishing. I stepped forward, muscles tensed, prepared to burst in if needed. Deep within me, I felt something new begin to form. A seed of something dangerous.

Mom's silhouette moved forward, hand on Wei's arm. *"Of course that's not it. You know I'm happy with... us. It's my ex. He has a temper. He's not sweet, like you."*

Wei sat up taller. *"I can protect you, Jia. I have resources now."*

"I know. But then you might get hurt, and I would never forgive myself. Please understand."

"I can take care of us."

"I know," Mom said, tone soothing. *"But tonight, let me take care of you."* She leaned forward and drew him into a kiss, hand trailing down his chest. He moaned softly.

I ran, the sounds of their foreplay trailing me down the hall. I didn't care where; anything to put distance between me and *that*. I gagged, tasting bile, but I kept moving.

It was dark; I could barely see more than a few feet ahead. Behind me, there was the sound of footsteps. Terror shot through me, and I picked up speed. *It couldn't be, it couldn't be him, why was he here? But he was here, he was after me. Ten years apart had only made him angrier. I knew if he found me, he would kill me. I had accepted gifts from him when I was young, when I first made my debut in the opera. We'd gone to dinner once, to keep my secret, and I'd broken it off. But his obsession only grew. And now he was here, and he had a knife, and I needed to find somewhere to hide, and...*

I stumbled, and then the floor beneath me vanished, and then I was falling, falling—

—I landed hard, back cracking on hard stone. My vision blurred as pain shot through my body, so intense I nearly passed out. My lungs labored, each breath bringing a fresh wave of agony. I couldn't cry out, couldn't do anything but scream internally and hope that this was the end.

Above me, something loomed. The shape was split, each half perfectly synchronized with the other. Double vision. No, they weren't exactly the same. One was a woman, face painted with a white opera mask, wearing an ornamented headdress with stylized horns. The other was inhuman, a twisted, rotting thing with twitching tendrils bursting from its skull.

It—they—reached down and took my hand with surprising tenderness, and the pain melted away. They lifted me, and my back was whole again, my body unbroken save a few muscle aches. My mind felt foggy.

I stared at the creature still holding my hand. With each blink, it—she—became more human, until I was looking into Deng Aili's face. She was much younger than in the photos; just a girl, like me, and more beautiful than anyone I'd ever seen. She stared at me with her wide, brown eyes, soft with understanding. My gaze traveled down to her thick, red lips. I felt like I knew her intimately, like I'd been living in her body. Like she understood me in a way no one ever had before.

I opened my mouth to thank her. Instead of words, a song emerged.

Aili joined me—she the melody, I the harmony. Together, we sang as she led me through a vast chamber with vaulted ceilings. Our song was ancient and true, each note gliding out with the ease of knowing. As if we were drawing upon the wisdom of the Opera House; the power of all those voices, all the starry-eyed girls who'd lived here, sang here, loved here. The girls who died here. Candles covered nearly every surface, dripping wax onto the cold stone. They were the only illumination; their flickering light cast strange shadows that made the room shift and warp with each step.

Aili led me to an alcove with a gorgeous wooden bed, lush with bright, silk sheets and an embroidered comforter. A mirror sat behind it, tall and intricate as the one in Kristy's room. We both sat down, and Aili turned to me, this time taking both my hands in hers. The look she gave me carried years of secrets and longing. I glanced into the mirror to see that I was in costume as well, dressed as one of the opera dancers. When I looked up again, she was still staring into my eyes with that intense, private gaze.

I nodded once, and her eyes turned hungry. She moved forward and closed the gap between us with a kiss so ferocious I felt like I was being devoured. Her hands dropped to my waist, and she began to undress me, and I slipped my fingers into her robes and followed suit. We had done this countless times; nothing felt more right with the world than when we were together. After years of hiding away, we had carved out this secret place for ourselves, and we had made it our own, over and over.

Aili pushed me back, gently, onto the bed. She was warm, her touch electric as her skin pressed into mine. With each movement, I recalled more of our moments together. We had grown up here, two girls plucked from different orphanages, sold to the Opera House. We had been the best of friends, and then we had bloomed into this.

I remembered our stolen kisses in dark corners; my jealousy as Aili let various men take her on dates, even though I knew she did it only to quell any dangerous rumors. The rich young man who had taken a fancy to her, bringing her flowers every night, vowing to make her his wife. I'd begged her not to accept his invitation, but she had done it for me, for us, promising it would be okay. As we watched the years pass, our traditional song and dance becoming yet another secret thing, he grew in importance in the Party. He gained power, and he took a wife, and I thought we were safe at last.

Until the day he showed up again at the opera.

All the love and beauty and terror of our lives together flashed through my mind as we brought each other pleasure with practiced motions. I knew what she liked, and I delighted in eliciting each gasp or moan or sighed whisper of my name. *Xuělì*. At last, she shuddered against me, and I against her, and we fell asleep in one another's arms, dreaming of a more merciful world.

CHAPTER 11

I woke in my own bed, skin tingling with remembered warmth, mind muddled. What the hell had happened the previous night? My head pounded, and I ached all over. Looking around, I couldn't see anything out of place. I was in yesterday's clothing, my outfit rumpled by sleep, and though my back was tender to the touch in places, there was no bruising.

I thought of Aili's fierce kiss, of everything we did after, and my cheeks grew hot. It had to be just a dream. But it'd been so vivid. And where had that name come from?

Xueli.

I remembered Aili's warm breath between my legs, her panting as I pulled off her lace panties, the taste of her on my tongue. My breaths quickened.

You have to understand how much this freaked me out. I didn't know the terms *demi* or *ace* yet, but I knew I'd never felt that way about anyone, never done anything like... that, before. The suddenness of my desire scared me more than anything else. I didn't know what the fuck was happening to me, and I was too embarrassed to talk to anyone about it, so I tried my best to shove down the panic and go about my day.

I was assigned to clean the auditorium with Mom. And though I didn't usually look forward to shifts, I was relieved by the prospect of a good distraction. I decided I must have had a weird, hallucinogenic reaction to something in the previous night's dinner, then shut that mental door tight and went to work.

When I saw Mom, I remembered the picture of her in the article, and her secret photo of Deng Aili. I wanted answers and drawing them out of her gave me something to focus on. Between that and the daunting task of cleaning the entire theater thoroughly before the evening performance, I could keep my mind occupied.

"Mom?" I mopped the stage floor, stepping over the spot where I'd stood and sang the previous night. In the daylight, the room felt completely different.

"Hm?" Mom looked lovely, framed by a square of light coming in from above. She bent down to fish out a piece of trash from under a wooden chair.

I chose my words carefully. "You grew up around here, right?"

She smiled. "Close by."

I wanted her in a good mood, so I asked more questions,

coaxing out what I could. As I listened, she conjured memories of her childhood, so vivid I felt them wrap around me. Mom, running in a pack with her cousins to collect hóngbāo on Lunar New Year. All of them comparing whose red envelope was filled with the most cash, amounts chosen by her năinai based on who was in favor. Lying on bamboo sleeping mats in the loft of her best friend's house, listening to Jay Chou croon through her CD player. Stuffing herself with long-life noodles and stewed eggs on every birthday.

She didn't mention the falling-out with her family when she ran away with her boyfriend at seventeen or the death of her parents in a car accident the following year. She never liked dwelling on difficult things. Sometimes I wondered if that's why she kept falling for men who were covered in bright red flags. She blocked out how bad things could get.

"Did you come here a lot as a kid, then?" I asked. "To Huihuang Opera House?"

Mom's hackles rose instantly, and I suppressed a sigh. Whenever I hoped she was about to relax about her past, something always triggered her defense system. "I told you I watched some shows. Lots of locals did."

"Okay, but..."

"Focus, Megan. We can't afford to be sloppy." The force of Mom's need to change the subject was a near-physical push.

I almost let it go, until I thought of her cherubic teenage face staring up at me from the photo in the article. Keeping my eyes down, I finished scrubbing the stage floor. "Did you ever work here?"

Though Mom didn't stop cleaning the seats, I felt tension radiate off her. "Why do you ask that?"

I swallowed. "I was curious how you knew Wei. That's all."

Her stare bored into the top of my head, and I kept my gaze fixed downward. Mom didn't answer for a moment, and a flash of annoyance hit me. I was sure she was about to spin a lie or half-truth.

"He was a friend from school," she said when she finally spoke again. "One of the few I stayed in touch with after moving to America." She left the rest unspoken—with my biological father and baby me in tow. Before he left us when I was just four years old.

I picked up my bucket and headed for the aisle near where Mom was cleaning up. "So, you never lived here before? Like we're doing now, in the servants' quarters?"

"What's come over you, Megan?" Mom asked. "You used to be such a guāi háizi."

I let out a frustrated sound, unable to stand tiptoeing around her sensibilities anymore. "Are you kidding me, Mom? I'm *always* good. I never push you to talk about anything you're uncomfortable with!"

"Megan! Keep your voice down."

"It's not rocket science! There's something you're not

telling me about that night you found me in the secret passageway. If you didn't work here or live here before, how did you know about the mirror in Kristy's room?"

Mom threw down her trash bag. "You were missing from your room, and I saw the light on in her room, just like you did!"

"No, you didn't! I found a picture of you here in 1997."

"What are you talking about?"

I made a frustrated sound. I wasn't saying any of this the right way. "There was an old article about the Opera House with a picture of a big group standing in front of it! You were in it. Were you a performer here?"

Mom faltered. "I... don't know what you're talking about. What's gotten into you lately? Why must you be so difficult?"

"*I'm* the difficult one?"

"I know the last few weeks have been hard, but I'm trying my best. I didn't punish you for snooping, and this is how you repay me? Stop inventing conspiracies. You're too old to let your imagination run wild like this. You should be making friends. I told you. You can borrow my makeup, and I'll fix up your hair. It's your best feature and you never do anything with it. You should be going out with people your age. You're old enough to date now, you know. You could meet someone cute and—"

"Mom! My friends are back in *Portland*, where you took me from. I went to school there. I was making friends before you dragged me away yet again. Look where we are. Look what we have to do just to live! And I don't *want* to date anyone. Not if it means my life will turn out like yours!"

Mom's face fell, and she burst into tears.

Regret hit, hard and instant. Mom looked frail and exhausted, and with the amount of makeup she had caked on, I knew her bruises hadn't fully faded. An apology sat on the tip of my tongue, nearly escaping.

I clenched my fists and pressed my lips shut, refusing to give her the satisfaction, reminding myself it was always like this. She never told me anything and then she made me feel bad for asking.

Mom turned and walked out of the auditorium, crying noisily. My heart sank. I hated this. I didn't know which was stronger: my guilt for making her cry, or my resentment that she would rather abandon me than be honest for once.

I watched her leave without turning back.

For a while, I rage-cleaned, fueled by how bad Mom would feel when she returned to find me doing the work she had signed us up for. I barely complained about having to work. I *always* understood. And I hadn't told Yi I worked as a cleaner. She knew some things about my life with Mom, but even she didn't know everything. I was forever protecting Mom.

I scrubbed the little decorative elements on the railing as angry thoughts ran wild through my mind.

I hated when Mom brought up dating. She always wanted

me to meet a cute boy—or maybe someone of another gender. For all that she'd grown up with rigid traditionalist Chinese values, I thought she'd be open-minded in that regard. But it wasn't about who I was attracted to, it was about how. At that age, I had only an inkling of how attraction worked for me, but it was enough to know how very different Mom and I were in that regard. And that difference, she couldn't seem to understand.

Mom used to pore over my yearbooks—even when I wasn't in them, having transferred in partway through the year—and ask me coyly what I thought of each person in my grade. I knew what she was fishing for, but I never knew quite how to respond.

While I'd found myself interested in the occasional person here and there, I'd never known any of them well enough to want to *do* anything with them. Not when I didn't feel connected to any of them, which I couldn't imagine happening until I had the chance to trust someone more fully. And how was I supposed to trust anyone when we moved away before I could ever reach that point? The only person I knew well enough to be attracted to in that way was Yi, and it had never been like that between us.

I didn't understand how Mom could give her body over so quickly to men she hadn't known long, and it wasn't only because they usually turned out to be sleazy. I had felt the same way when Yi mentioned casual hookups or when I watched shows where characters had one-night stands. The whole idea of desiring that kind of intimacy with someone you only know on a surface level just didn't make sense to me.

And honestly, I wouldn't have minded trying on makeup or letting Mom style my hair occasionally. But I knew she wouldn't stop there. If Mom saw an opening, she'd have rushed toward it. By then, she must have had some inkling that I was different from her, but she'd never bothered to ask or tried to understand. Instead, she kept pushing, as if by finally hooking up with someone, I'd somehow understand why she kept dragging us to different places for the sake of her latest man.

I tell you all this now because I want you to know that identity isn't always clear-cut and easy to sort. I want you to know not everything is a matter of who you are or aren't attracted to, that it can take time to figure out. I wish I could explain this all to you on some distant day, over custard tarts and warm tea. Instead, this will have to do.

I wasn't sure when the tears began to fall, but my cheeks were damp with them. Why was it that Mom would rather spend her free time flirting with men like Wei than sit down and have a real conversation with me, her only daughter? And why did I always have to be the one to apologize or let things go?

I understand, now, that Mom must have been overwhelmed by our situation, by the weight of all the decisions she'd made for us. By the path our lives had taken, spiraling ever faster toward a future where we had nothing for ourselves, nothing left of ourselves; a pair of rabbits perpetually at the mercy of ever-hungrier wolves.

I understand, and I'm not certain the knowing of it changes anything.

In my frustration, I scrubbed so hard that I accidentally scratched the paint off the surface I'd been cleaning. I stopped, feeling rotten. It wasn't the theater's fault I had issues with Mom.

"I'm sorry," I whispered, brushing the damaged spot with tenderness.

It was clear by then that Mom wasn't coming back. I felt drained—of fight, of anger, of energy. I left the cart of cleaning supplies in the theater and walked out. She could deal with the fallout if anyone was angry.

I considered walking around the courtyard, but I didn't want to risk running into Mom or any of the other cleaners.

With nothing better to do, I headed to my room. I leaned against the wall beside my bed and picked the book up off the floor where I'd dropped it the night before. I opened the page, afraid my stomach would rebel. Thankfully, neither the nausea nor the sickly-sweet taste returned.

I took a deep breath and read on.

In a small chamber of the cave, the gleaming white sleeves of Baigujing's best robes grazed her stone vanity table as she watched herself in the mirror, refreshing the rouge on her lips. Tonight's feast was to be her moment of triumph. She would look her best when it was finally time to taste Tang Sanzang's flesh and ascend to immortality. She smiled, revealing a full set of sharpened teeth, perfectly shaped to rend flesh.

When she was satisfied with her presentation for the evening, Baigujing tended the stoneware pot over a roaring flame in the back of the cavern, heating the rich broth she would stew the monk in. As she neared the captives, Sha Wujing moaned, begging to be let free, but Tang Sanzang remained silent, head bowed in prayer. Baigujing leaned down to swipe her thumb against Sha Wujing's cheek.

"Don't worry," she said, grinning just wide enough for him to see the reflection of the flames in her teeth. "You'll die quickly, once you're in."

Sha Wujing thrashed as Baigujing walked away, thinking of how well the flavor of fish would complement her stew.

In groups, the guests began to arrive. Demons with sunken blue faces, gray claws for hands, and black pools for eyes. Demons with skin redder than blood, black manes like horses, and horns like those of a bull. Demons who could snort flames from their nostrils and kick up wind with their hooves. From far and wide they came, lured by the promise of flesh.

Baigujing let them all enter.

The last guest, an older demon, hobbled in.

"Where are your guards?" Baigujing asked her friend, for she was known to travel with an escort now that her prime was past.

The demon shook her head. "They were killed by the Monkey King, but they bought me time to escape."

At the mention of her nemesis, Baigujing snarled. "We will take our vengeance upon him after the feast. Come, come, I have something to show you."

Baigujing led her elderly guest toward the back, showing her the two captives tied up beside the stew pot. She went to stir the pot one more time, taking in the delicious scent. It was time.

She turned around and was startled to find her friend gone. In the old demon's place was Sun Wukong, who had unveiled his disguise. Realizing she had been deceived, Baigujing let out an enraged screech just as the Monkey King attacked. Most of her fellow demons fled, having heard tales of Sun Wukong's feats.

In her center of power, so close to her heart's greatest desire, Baigujing was not easily defeated. But at last, the legendary golden-banded staff, gifted to Sun Wukong by the Dragon King, was more than the demon could handle. Her preferred form fell away, leaving only her true shape: a skeleton with gaping eye sockets and teeth like daggers. She lunged for Sun Wukong, mouth open, jaw ready to clamp down.

The Monkey King swung his staff, landing one last, fatal blow.

Baigujing crumpled to the ground, lifeless.

Sun Wukong fought off the remaining demons. When the last was defeated, he freed his master and fellow disciple. He told them how Zhu Bajie had found him after escaping the cave and given warning. Sun Wukong had rushed there to save his master, killing an evil old demon and her guards before donning her form as a disguise.

Once the demons were defeated, Tang Sanzang and Sun Wukong reconciled. The four pilgrims pressed on westward to complete their journey.

As I set the book down, dissatisfaction soured my mood further. Even though Baigujing was the obvious villain, I felt a pang of sympathy for her. All that work for her goal, horrendous as it was, and she never got to taste her victory.

What a fucking waste.

CHAPTER 12

I walked down the hall with purpose. If I thought too hard, I'd chicken out. It felt like ages before I reached the room near the back of the Opera House. Like the performers' rooms, it had a screen door built of carved wood and rice paper.

I knocked.

The door slid open to reveal Wei, clearly surprised to see me. His face split into a grin. "Megan! What can I do for you? Do you want to borrow my computer again?"

It was almost too much; I ached to turn and run, but I forced myself to smile back. "Can we talk?"

"Of course, yes! Come in."

Forcing down my trepidation, I nodded and stepped inside.

Wei kept his office tidy. The wall was full of accolades and photos of him at fancy events, standing with important-looking people, each picture framed in gold. I wrinkled my nose reflexively before remembering I was here to play nice.

Once we were both seated, I nodded at a photo of Mom on his desk. "Can I see that?"

He smiled, handing it over. "Your mom was a beauty."

"She still is." I inspected the photo. Mom looked around my age. Her face was tilted up to the sky, exposing her swanlike neck. She had her eyes closed, and a gentle smile sat on her lips.

"Yes, that's what I meant. She *is* beautiful. I need to get a recent photo of her framed. Of the three of us. That would be good. We should all take a photo together!"

"Yeah, sure." I couldn't stop staring. Mom looked uncaged, unburdened. "When was this taken?"

"Right after she moved into the Opera House, I believe," Wei said.

I looked up sharply, mind racing. "When she... Right. Of course." I couldn't let on that she hadn't told me, or he'd clam up. "What was she like back then?"

"Popular. All the boys were in love with her." Wei blushed. "The first time I saw Jia, she was surrounded by admirers. Some of them were... not kind to me."

"Why?"

Wei shrugged. "I was the theater manager's son. I was a few years younger than them. I was an easy target. I don't know."

I studied him, surprised by his frankness.

"People don't always like me at first," he said. "But Jia was nice. She did not have to be. She could have been cruel when

I brought her flowers I picked from my ma's garden. Instead, she thanked me and wore one in her hair all day."

I could picture them. Wei, twelve or thirteen, with a bowl cut, a bouquet, and a hopeful heart. Mom, sixteen or seventeen, gorgeous and cool, seated on the stage, surrounded by flirty boys. Mom might be difficult, but she was kind and friendly, too. And she assumed the best intentions in everyone. Sometimes I thought that was her downfall.

"That sounds like Mom," I agreed. "Did you invite her to live here in the Opera House back then?"

"Oh, no!" Wei laughed. "I barely knew her before she moved in."

"So, you didn't know her through school?"

"No. She wasn't from this district. We never went to the same school."

Beneath the table, I clenched my fists, trying not to let my hurt show. I couldn't think of a single reason Wei would lie about this. He genuinely seemed to want me to like him. Mom was the one who lied to me when it suited her. That's why I was here, after all. She was never honest about her past, so I'd had to find another source.

That didn't lessen the pain.

"Right. I get mixed up sometimes," I said.

"It must all seem so far away for you." Wei laughed. "You're so young, and it was another lifetime. But it feels like just yesterday for me. Jia moved in with one of the performers."

He eyed me, as if I didn't know how Mom was. "Don't think poorly of her. You know what her father was like."

I froze. I had no idea what he was talking about, but I tried to sound nonchalant. "I've heard this and that."

Wei shook his head. "Awful man. He came storming in once, demanding to see his daughter. I don't know how he found out where she'd gone. She stayed hidden, and my parents convinced him she wasn't here. Even after he left, none of us could find her for hours. Maybe Huihuang Opera House hid her."

"Wait. What do you mean it hid her?" My mind reeled. I remembered the previous night—running down the corridor, heart racing, while footsteps sounded behind me. It had felt like a memory.

"Do you know what huīhuáng means?"

I felt my cheeks flush as I shook my head. I hated when people pointed out words I didn't know. Hated that I cared.

"It means splendid, or glorious. And that's what you see on the outside. Back when it was constructed, this place was the tallest building for kilometers around. It was a symbol of pride, of culture and power. Troupes would travel across the country just to perform on this stage. Because of that, the living quarters were built. Huihuang Opera House was responsible for so many people who were far from home. It takes that responsibility seriously."

"You talk about it like it's a living thing."

"Let me show you something." Wei pulled a binder off the shelf behind him and flipped through it. "Here, look." He set it down in front of me.

Scrawled Chinese text accompanied sketches of the Opera House, along with floorplans and diagrams. "Blueprints?"

"Plans for the Opera House, yes. These are reproductions. The originals are delicate, so we keep them in storage." He pointed to various rooms in the floorplan. "This is the main theater, the shrine, and the ticket office. These are the back rooms. This wing is the living quarters. And this is where we are now."

It looked so much smaller than the Opera House felt. "Why are you showing me this?"

"Over the years, there have been many rumors. Doors opening to rooms where none should be. Hallways that can never be found again. Impossible twists and turns that simply cannot exist according to this." Wei tapped the binder.

I thought of a bone-white hand beckoning to me from the auditorium entrance. Of the angry voices I'd followed down an endless-seeming corridor. Falling into the chamber below.

A chill ran through me. But no, that had been a dream, a hallucination, the product of a tired mind. "Maybe you have a mold problem. When we first arrived, you said some part of the Opera House is always rotting. Some spores can cause delusions." I tried to sound confident.

"Maybe," he conceded. "But I've spent my whole life here.

I've heard stories, read tales. And I've been a child wandering its halls. Those secret places seem to open for people when they need it most. I think Huihuang Opera House loves the lost and the lonely. It takes care of them."

I wondered if that was why Mom and I were here. If she, too, thought of the Opera House as a safe haven. "Interesting."

Wei took my response for skepticism, and a defensive note crept into his voice. "It may sound silly to you, but there *is* something special about this place. Many world-class performers began here. A famous opera singer named Deng Aili—she was the first. Then there was Tán Xuělì, a dancer, and the violinist Chen Guoliang. They were all—"

"Wait, who was the second one?"

"Tan Xueli?"

"Yes. The name sounds familiar." I remembered Deng Aili's whisper in my ear and shivered.

"Would you like to see her perform?"

I blinked. "She's... here?"

Wei laughed. "No. We have videos of her in our archive." Several keyboard clicks later, he flipped his screen around. Xueli looked not much older than me, petite and graceful in a colorful costume and makeup. I watched her perform a solo dance, each whirl or twirl as effortless as if she were a fae creature from a long-forgotten tale.

I couldn't tear my gaze away. "She's talented." It was an understatement.

"She was."

"Was? Where is she now?" Even as I asked, I knew what he'd say.

Wei shifted, looking uneasy. "No one knows for sure. The government here... well. It's not a bad place to live. I'm sure in America you hear horror stories about us. But Beijing is beautiful. Rich with history, and a center for the arts. I mean what I said about singing lessons. It would be no trouble to arrange them for you."

"That's not necessary."

Wei looked hurt. "I know, but..."

"We don't need your charity." It was a ridiculous thing to say, but he didn't call me out.

"I don't see it that way. Megan... I know this must be hard for you, being here. And I know you have no reason to trust me. But I love your mom. I've loved her all my life. She was kind to me when no one else was. Before I had anything to offer anyone. She didn't care about that. I've spent years hoping she would move back here. I know her memories of her childhood still hurt. But I think she could begin to heal here. I really believe in Huihuang Opera House. I think it could be a fresh start for both you and Jia. For all of us."

He sounded so earnest that I couldn't help looking up. As if I could measure a person that way. He offered me a light smile, and I felt myself soften a tiny bit.

"You really love Mom."

"I really love your mom. Having her here is a dream come true. I want both of you to be happy here." He hesitated, then nodded to himself as if he'd decided something. "Keep this," he said, giving me the framed photo of Mom.

"Thanks," I whispered, clutching it tight as I left his office.

On the way back to my room, Wei's words rang in my head, repeating themselves like a refrain.

You know what her father was like.

I felt like such a fool. Mom had begun painting the picture of her childhood as idyllic ages ago, and I'd never thought to question it. I'd always figured her reticence to talk about her parents was because of the car crash; that she'd never gotten over losing them. But it was all a fantasy. Of course it was. I couldn't believe I'd fallen for it.

Wei assumed I knew. It hadn't occurred to him that Mom might have kept it from me. He thought he understood her. In a way, Wei reminded me of Mom, the two of them determined to see the best in one another.

I flopped back on my bed, head spinning as I rewrote the tale Mom had told. I didn't think she'd lied about everything, but she plucked only the prettiest memories to show me, snatching them away before I could see the cracks.

Now, I wove those moments into my understanding of Mom, uncovering the layers behind rosy recollections she'd shared. Her frequent sleepovers at various friends' houses. The time she'd mentioned how her mom liked to take her on fun, impromptu trips. Her secretiveness, and the way she dissociated whenever things got rough with one of her boyfriends.

Mom had spoken of running away from home a year before the crash, but she'd always made it sound like a youthful flight of fancy. I'd believed her. I'd thought her relationships and the mess she'd turned our lives into had been a result of her guilt over abandoning her family—only to have them die thinking she didn't love them, or something like that. But it had begun so much earlier, hadn't it?

I turned on my side, staring at nothing as the minutes ticked by. Was Wei right about Mom and Beijing? Her packing up and running had started here. What if being here was the first step in helping her heal?

Sighing, I sat up, and my eyes caught on the copy of *Xiyouji* Wei had brought me. I picked it up, flipping through it absently. Would I be able to read these words someday, if Mom and I stayed long enough?

Someone had doodled around the edges of the pages. I snorted. You'd think with the wealth Wei liked to flaunt, he could've at least brought me a new copy.

The drawings were cute and playful, done in a cartoonish style. I smiled as I looked through them. Sun Wukong eating all the peaches of immortality. Sun Wukong and Guanyin. Sun Wukong laying on the ground, tongue out and Xs over his eyes. They were interspersed with handwritten blocks of Chinese text, surrounded by little hearts and clouds.

I frowned. Something about the writing and the hearts looked familiar. They were intentionally lopsided, and a few of them had little faces in them. Lips pursed, I turned to the title page.

佳

I didn't know many hànyǔ characters, but this one I recognized. Jia. This book had been Mom's. These were her drawings.

I didn't know what to feel as I started over from the beginning, looking for her doodles. Wei must have kept this little piece of Mom's history all these years. I blinked back tears, wishing she'd been the one to share it with me.

I tried to imagine what it would be like to live here, in Mom's hometown. Once we got more settled in, would she start taking me to visit places from her childhood? What if, eventually, she showed me where her home had been? She talked about her cousins, her āyí and nǎinai, but she never explained why she no longer spoke with them, why I'd never met any of them. If we stayed, would she seek them out again?

I thought about having a family—a real, extended family beyond me and Mom—and my heart hurt. Usually, I was good about never quite letting myself succumb to hope. But I couldn't stop the *what ifs* from whirling around my mind, kicking up long-buried dreams.

I set the photo of Mom and her copy of *Xiyouji* on my side table and dug up the top Kristy had bought me. I put it on and looked in the mirror, imagining myself living here for real. Taking lessons; maybe making friends I could meet up with. I could almost taste it; a life here for me and Mom. One that was full. Genuine.

As I stared at my reflection, my white shirt began to lengthen into a robe with billowing sleeves, blue thread weaving itself around the edges into swirling embroidery in serpentine patterns. My lips stung as they reddened, nails growing and blackening. My scalp itched as a metal crown sprouted atop my head, two feathers bursting forth and lengthening, amidst a sea of growing white pom-poms. I reached for the base of the crown, unsurprised to find there was no seam between it and me.

Instinctively, I began to sing, and my voice came out rich and full-bodied. It was mine, but it was more. With each inhale, I felt the power of the Opera House enter my lungs. With each exhale, I gifted its beauty, its pain, its love, and its rage to the world.

Someone knocked, and I turned. When I looked back in the mirror, I was me again.

I slid the door open a crack. In the hallway, Haozhe waved. "Hi Megan!"

"Hi?" I'd seen various troupe members around, but I hadn't spoken with Haozhe since that first awkward meeting. His moniker for me still lived rent-free in my mind. *American girl.*

"I heard you singing! You're *really* good."

"Thanks?"

Haozhe's grin faltered. "Yeah. I know that first day you were here was, uh, a little weird. I wasn't trying to... I don't hit on..." He reddened. "This is not going well, is it."

I raised an eyebrow.

"Let me start over. I've been feeling bad about how we treated you. I was trying to be friendly, but I think I made things worse. I meant to find you earlier to apologize. And welcome you. It's been busy! Then I was walking down the hall and heard you singing, and now we're here."

"Are you always this..."

"...weird? Embarrassing? Handsome?"

I couldn't help cracking a smile. "Sure, if you say so."

He grinned. "We're going out for karaoke after the show. Want to join?"

"Karaoke? After a whole evening of performing?"

"Yeah! We're singers, you know."

I rolled my eyes. "I don't think Siquan is going to like that."

Haozhe rolled his eyes. "I doubt he even remembers. That whole day is probably a blur to him."

"That seems... bad?"

"We're working on getting him help. But he won't care, I promise."

"Why are you suddenly being so nice?" I couldn't help myself. I didn't want to walk into some kind of elaborate prank.

I expected Haozhe to shrug off my question or offer a flippant explanation. Instead, his face morphed into the most serious expression I'd seen from him yet. He looked at me, and for a moment, I felt like I could see something beyond his playful, outgoing persona. "A lot of the others here come from money. The training we go through is expensive. But the theater has this scholarship program for kids like me. They're the reason I'm here."

"Wait. You mean Wei?"

"Well, his parents started it, but yeah. He expanded it, and he still runs it. All of us get free room and board in the Opera House."

"Okay..."

"I'm just saying. Talent and potential should matter. And not only when you're rich as fuck. If you can sing like that, the theater will fund your lessons. I know it sounds stupid, but being part of the troupe changed my life."

"I've never really thought about it." The lie tasted bitter on my tongue.

"You don't have to join." Haozhe shrugged. "But forget all that. Come to karaoke. Kristy said you're cool, and she's smarter than the rest of us."

"That, I believe."

Haozhe burst out laughing. "So that's a..."

"Yeah. I'll join." I smiled.

Haozhe cheered and skipped off dramatically.

I watched him disappear around a corner, feeling lighter than I had in a while.

CHAPTER 13

That evening, I got ready to watch the opera with Mom. I was still wearing the shirt Kristy had bought for me—if Mom asked, I'd say it was borrowed. The fabric was soft, and through some magic of engineering, it draped perfectly no matter how I moved. My clothing wouldn't be as fancy as many of the evening show guests', but I did my best, pairing the shirt with my old black ballet flats and a skirt I'd dug up in the lost and found.

I tucked the copy of *Xiyouji* in my bag like a talisman. Maybe I'd show Mom, maybe I wouldn't. I hadn't seen her since our fight, and I wasn't sure how awkward tonight would be.

When Mom picked me up at my room in a silky green dress and peacock earrings, she seemed in a rare good mood. I decided to go with it. We hadn't seen a show together since she and Dad had split up. Despite everything, I was looking forward to my first time seeing Beijing opera live.

By the time we arrived, the energy in the auditorium was spirited and anticipatory—loud with chatter from a full house of guests. Tucked stage-right in the back corner, the orchestra played an upbeat, welcoming melody. Mom pointed out various Chinese instruments, offering analogies to ones I was more familiar with. The yuèqín, or moon guitar, was like a banjo with fewer strings. The bright, lively dízi was a bamboo flute with holes instead of keys. It was like having her translate a story for me. I soaked up every word.

Mom handed an usher our tickets, and he led us up a rickety staircase to a pair of seats in box five. This spot *had* to be expensive.

"Is Wei coming too?" I asked.

"No. He asked if he could join, but I thought it would be fun to do something just the two of us."

"And he didn't mind?"

"Of course not." Mom passed me a set of binoculars.

Just the two of us tonight. Some of the tension released from my body. I looked over; I hadn't seen Mom this dressed up since before we'd fled the apartment. The light flattered her, smoothing out her skin and softening her features. She looked beautiful and mysterious; I thought of the old photo of Mom that Wei had given me.

Biting my lip, I reached into my bag and pulled out her old copy of *Xiyouji*. "Mom?"

"Hm?"

"I think this was yours."

She drew in a sharp breath. I gave it to her, and she opened the cover, moving as if under an enchantment. Her eyes traveled to her name, penned alongside a Sun Wukong doodle. "How did you find this?"

"Wei gave it to me."

She nodded slowly, not taking her eyes off the book. "This was mine when I was your age. I never thought I'd see it again."

I wanted to ask her about her dad, about living here, about everything, but I forced myself to be patient. She held onto the book as the lights dimmed, drawing our attention.

The crowd hushed as stage lights blazed to life. Red curtains opened to reveal Sun Wukong wearing a gold costume I recognized from the wardrobe room. He carried a staff; after a short opening song, he twirled it to the rhythm of cymbals. I hadn't caught the name of the actor, but he was just as roguishly playful as he'd been the day I'd met the troupe. He wore the furry monkey mask I recognized, but this time, his face was covered in white and red makeup, shaping his features into those of the Monkey King.

The actor's commitment to the character was flawless. I looked through the binoculars to see him twitching his eyes and lips in micro motions synced with percussive beats, each action exaggerated by his dramatic makeup. Through playful expressions and movements, he conveyed Sun Wukong's mischievousness.

Though I couldn't understand most of the words, sung as they were in a drawn out, stylized way, it hardly mattered. I watched the choreographed dances as Mom whispered in my ear, sharing various background details about Chinese opera. I couldn't tell if she was in a chatty mood or if this was her way of apologizing. Either way, I felt myself thaw, warmed by her full attention. Maybe Mom did know what I needed, after all.

She told me each costume was a unique work of art, each piece handmade and often hand embroidered, the more intricate outfits showcasing hundreds of hours of labor. She explained the four archetypal characters of Chinese opera and what made them distinct.

Shēng, the male role, was often a prince or young scholar garbed in robes with flowing water sleeves, though they could also be an old man or warrior. Dàn, the female role, encompassed numerous subcategories; Mom's favorite type was huādàn, the lively maiden with rouge-lined eyes and an elaborate coiffure. Jìng, the painted face character, used bold makeup to indicate its personality traits—white paint for craftiness and treachery, black paint for uprightness and impartiality. Chǒu, the clown, served as comic relief, with features exaggerated by makeup or a white patch around the nose and eyes.

While the archetypes had traditionally been assigned specific genders, the performers playing them could be anyone—the famed Queen of Beijing Opera was a man known best for his role as the legendary Bái Sùzhēn, Madame White Snake.

It was my favorite thing, seeing Mom like this. In her element.

Even though I'd just read the story, I let her tell me about Sun Wukong and Baigujing. I wanted to envelop myself in the warmth of her storytelling. I wanted every moment to be like this, with Mom focusing on me, telling me something she could only have learned during her years in Beijing.

In my mind, I heard the echo of Wei's words. *I think she could begin to heal here.* Already, she was opening up about her past in a way she'd never done before.

I missed Portland, but I would have missed it less if I'd had this mom all the time.

"That's Zhu Bajie." Mom pointed to a performer in the oversized pig mask, resting on a huge prop rock.

"I remember him from the stories you used to tell me about Sun Wukong. It's cool seeing them come to life."

Mom smiled. "You don't mind the music or singing style? Wei tells me even Chinese kids these days don't always appreciate the beauty in it. Western theater styles and pop songs have become so ubiquitous that traditional Beijing opera feels more foreign to many of them."

"It took getting used to. But now I think it's pretty cool."

Mom hugged me. "That's my girl."

I leaned into her shoulder. After a minute or two sitting in companionable silence, I glanced over, watching her watch the opera. She looked happy. I gathered my courage. "Mom?"

"Yes, Megan?"

"Who's Deng Aili?"

Mom stiffened, pulling away, and my heart dropped. Of course. I hadn't waited long enough. Once again, I'd ruined the mood.

"I think she was an opera singer who used to perform here," Mom said, tone cautious and even.

"I saw a photo of her in the theater shrine."

"Oh!" Mom's shoulders relaxed. "Yes, she was quite striking, wasn't she?"

"Yeah." I hesitated, knowing I was risking Mom closing up again, but I knew I'd never get a better chance than this. Swallowing hard, I pushed forward. "Didn't you used to have a photo of her?"

In the split-second pause between beats, I heard Mom's sharp inhale. "No, you must be misremembering."

"What? No, I remember you taking it out sometimes and looking at it." And always hiding it once she'd spotted me.

Mom shook her head, waving toward the stage. "Hey, pay attention. This is one of my favorite parts, where Baigujing is first introduced."

A group of actors appeared from the mist, waving flags and flanking a silhouetted figure. The demon-guards parted as a spotlight shone, illuminating Baigujing in an unearthly glow.

In her flowing white robes, Kristy was stunning as she swayed with the beat, singing a haunting tune. Her voice filled the theater like she was channeling three centuries of singers, most long dead, through every note. The entire Opera House came alive with her voice. Kristy sang the way I imagined a mermaid of ancient mythology might have sung; with an impossible resonance that could awaken an ancient monster from the depths.

Warm breath heated my neck, tickling the fine hairs, and a melodic voice whispered in my ear, words too soft to catch.

I whipped my head around. There was no one but me and Mom in the box. She was transfixed, eyes glazed over as she watched Kristy's performance. I glanced around at the other patrons to see if anyone else was acting like they'd heard something strange. It was difficult to make out expressions in the darkness of the theater, but as I watched each group, I realized that no one was moving at all. No shifting; no cries from small children or whispers from the audience. Not even a cough filled the air, as if time had stopped for everyone but me and the performers.

Through the strangeness, I couldn't help but wonder what it would be like to command stillness from an entire room with your song alone.

The melodic voice whispered again. This time I caught the last word.

Yours.

And I was onstage, singing. I was the embodiment of the Opera House, its mouthpiece, centuries of talent and ambition and desperation and power—raw, beautiful, delicious power—pumping through my veins, warming every hollow place within me. It built up in my lungs, and I channeled it into the auditorium, into the soft, fleshy hearts of my rapt audience.

I knew how incredible I sounded, like soaring hope and childhood dreams and a lifetime of promise. I would be the recipient of all the power and money and influence the Opera House held. Soon, I would reap my rewards.

Sun Wukong leapt forward with a snarl, slicing open my cheek with Jingu Bang, which should have been blunt, but it was sharp, bladed, wrong, and when his eyes met mine, I realized it was him, it was *him*, and panic coursed through me, sudden and fierce. I took off running, fueled by terror and the desire of the Opera House. Huihuang had kept me safe all my life, kept us both safe, and I trusted it more than anyone; more than myself. I ran, and I could feel his footsteps behind me, loud and insistent and too fast.

He caught up to me and grabbed my robes. I screamed and shoved him, and my fabric tore, a silky white piece still clutched in his greedy hands. Every moment between us flashed through my mind; all those gifts he'd sent that were not gifts but installments, each payment entitling him to ownership over one more piece of me. I hadn't understood this was his bargain, but now it didn't matter. He was here and he had a wife and he was important now and ten long years had passed, yet none of it mattered, none at all.

The corridor was dark, but I didn't need to know where I was going. I only needed to trust in the Opera House.

"Jiùmìng!" My voice came out half scream, half breathless cry, but it was enough.

A door opened, and I hurtled through, slamming it shut in his face. He pounded and screamed curses at me and tears ran down my face as I ran for the tucked away little corner of the chamber; for our secret place, the one the Opera House had made for Xueli and me because it loved us, because it wanted to keep us safe, because we were its treasures.

I crawled beneath the bed where we'd made love countless times, and I cowered, waiting for him to give up and leave, for someone to find him and take him away. Tears soaked my robes now, and I stifled the screams that threatened to tear from my throat.

I could still hear him shouting and kicking the door, and my body shuddered with each blow; if he found a way in, I would be the target of his rage.

Another voice cut through the air, feminine and angry. Dread flooded me. No. It couldn't be. She shouldn't be here. Why was she here?

"Nǐ duì Àilì zuòle shénme!" Xueli screamed. I could hear the note of panic behind her fierce words.

She was on the wrong side of the door.

As I scrambled out of my hiding place, my headdress caught on the bedframe, yanking it from my head and tearing a chunk of my hair with it. My scalp burned something fierce, and I screamed; I felt hot blood drip from the wound, soaking into my skin. Still, I ran toward her.

I could picture my dancer, standing as tall as her short frame would allow, protecting me. Terrified but forcing herself to be brave out of love. I could imagine his rage at being challenged. It would take only a moment for him to break her legs so she would never dance again. For him to stab her repeatedly in the chest, each time another chance to puncture her heart or lungs. To wrap his arms around her neck and squeeze until her muscles grew limp, all her promise seeping out in minutes; him, all the while, imagining she was me.

Life and love were so fragile, every day precious when you had everything in the world to lose. I could not let him hurt Xueli, whose only crime was to love me.

I grabbed a vase and flung the door open, ready to hit him over the head.

She was between me and him, and when she saw me, costume torn up, blood dripping, she screamed. "Aili!"

He shoved her out of the way and lunged for me, and my hastily constructed plan was for naught as he entered the secret room, snarling as he threw himself on me. I dropped the vase, and it shattered, and then Xueli was clawing at him, trying to pry him off. She'd never been more beautiful.

I whispered a prayer beneath my breath, too quiet for either of them to hear. *Please protect her. I'll do anything for you.*

The floor beneath Xueli opened, and she screamed as she dropped through. When it closed, leaving me and him alone in the chamber, I knew I wouldn't escape this last confrontation alive.

But I trusted in Huihuang Opera House, and I had saved her, after all. I was terrified; but I was relieved, too. Now I would pay the price.

"Nǐ yībèizi dōu shǔyú wǒ," he spat, hands gripping me hard enough to bruise.

I shook my head. He was wrong. I would never belong to him.

He smiled. "Nǐ yǐhòu bùzhǔn zài jùjué wǒ!" He slammed my head back against the floor and pressed his meaty hands over my face. I fought, but my head rang, and I was dizzy, and he was too strong. He pried my lips apart and pulled a knife from his belt and reached in and—

Blood, metallic and thick, filled my mouth, spilling out, spilling everywhere while I choked and gagged, and in the end, his last words to me were a sentence, for he made sure I could never, ever tell him no again.

I screamed, disoriented. I grabbed at my mouth, frantically felt for my tongue, awash with the relief of its presence. It was there, I was me, none of it had been real. My throat felt dry, and tears streamed down my face as I forced myself to go through breathing exercises to calm down.

Beside me, Mom's attention remained fixed on the

performance. Around us, the theater was silent, still. No one had heard me.

I watched through blurred vision as my heartbeat slowly returned to normal.

Kristy finished and sank to the floor in a graceful movement. Claps filled the air; everyone was acting normal again. It had felt so vivid, but it seemed no time had passed.

"Isn't she wonderful?" Mom's eyes glistened. She kissed me on the forehead and then leaned back away. "That was such a powerful performance."

"Yeah," I whispered. "Powerful."

CHAPTER 14

The curtains fell and opened again, revealing the cast. As the crowd applauded, they bowed low, then parted in the middle, forming an aisle. The actor playing Sun Wukong somersaulted up the path to cheers. And then Kristy was walking up the aisle. At the sight of her, everyone in the audience stood, as if in one coordinated motion, and burst into raucous shouting and applause. The Monkey King and the White Bone Demon joined hands, bowing low.

Both their bow and standing ovation lasted past the point of oddity, well into the range of uncomfortable. When they finally lifted their heads again, I gasped. Kristy's features had changed. In her place, I stared at Deng Aili.

"Mom, do you see..."

"Kristy is wonderful, isn't she?"

Mom wasn't looking at me. Her eyes were still trained on the stage. Aili twirled and bowed low again. I glanced around, but no one else seemed to notice anything odd. They were all as absorbed as Mom; even the children seemed wholly enthusiastic, shouting and cheering as they clapped along with everyone.

When the curtain closed for the final time and people began filing out of the theater, Mom turned to me. "Ready?"

"Yeah. But didn't you..." I trailed off, unsure how to explain. Where to begin? Had it been a daydream? A hallucination? Neither felt like the right word. It had the vividness and detail of a memory. I had *been* Aili. Mom had to know something. She hadn't wanted to talk about the photo, but if I confessed what had been happening to me, maybe she'd relent. "Actually, Mom?"

"Hm?" She was tucking *Xiyouji* into her bag.

"Can we talk? Just the two of us?"

"Of course!"

"Kristy said the teahouse is open late on show nights."

Mom stopped. "Oh. You mean right now?"

"Yeah. I just... I don't know if I'm okay."

She studied me, clearly going through some kind of internal debate. I felt like I had that first night we'd arrived, when I'd wanted her to tell Wei that she and I would share a room. Like I had when she'd first told me we were moving to China, and I'd begged her to keep us in Portland. *Please, Mom. Just this once.*

The moment Mom decided, I knew; she plastered on a bright grin, and my heart sank. "First thing tomorrow morning, okay? We'll get breakfast together before work!"

I opened my mouth, then shut it again, trailing her out of the theater wordlessly. The Mom who had explained Beijing opera to me was already gone. I didn't think I could bear one more excuse.

The foyer was densely packed; people buying souvenirs, parents wrangling hyper children, groups huddled together in animated conversation.

In the center of the room, a crowd had formed around someone, snapping photos and holding up items to sign, shouting, while a group of burly security guards did their best to hold them back. I thought they were surrounding Kristy. But when the guards managed to push enough people back for me to catch a glimpse, I saw that it was Joon-Ho at the center, looking as cool as he did on every one of Yi's photocards. He must have flown in for tonight's show.

Mom spotted Wei, who waved at her.

"Hey," Mom said to me. "Come with us."

"No, thanks."

"He's not so bad, I promise. He really wants to make this work. For all of us."

I didn't have the heart to tell her that he wasn't the reason I didn't want to go. "I know, Mom. It's okay. Breakfast tomorrow."

She worried her lip. "Maybe you shouldn't be here alone."

"I won't be. The cast invited me to karaoke afterward."

Mom's face lit up. "That's wonderful! Oh! Um. Here."

She handed me a few crumpled bills from her purse. Spending money from Wei, I guessed.

I forced a smile. "Thanks. Have fun."

She hugged me. "Tomorrow, I promise." When she let go, I felt bereft without her warmth. She wove her way through the crowd, greeting Wei with a kiss. Then, his hand on the small of her back, he escorted her outside, where they disappeared into a waiting car.

I was still staring through the window, out into the darkness, when someone leaned an elbow on my shoulder.

"Megan!"

I smiled. "Hi, Haozhe. Shouldn't you be signing shit for your adoring fans?"

"Oh, no one cares about me. They're here for the K-pop heartthrob. And, you know, the important people." He gestured at a corner where I recognized the actor playing Sun Wukong signing programs.

I shuddered, recalling Sun Wukong's leer as he slammed me—Aili—against the wall.

"You okay?"

"Yeah, I'm fine. Where's Kristy?"

He frowned. "She disappeared after the show."

"I'll go find her."

Haozhe's response was interrupted by a little girl who came up, smiling, and asked if he would sign her program. As he squatted to talk to her, I left, heading for the living quarters.

Kristy's light was on, her silhouette visible through the screen door. I reached out to knock but stopped when I heard her talking to someone.

"Wǒ ài nǐ, Bà."

Our first conversation had been about our missing dads. Why was she talking to hers now? I didn't see any other silhouettes.

It should have been impossible to tell what was happening through the grainy screen, and yet I could feel it, as though the Opera House wanted me to know, sharpening each shadow and opening my mind just enough for understanding. Kristy lifted a paper to her lips and kissed it. She set it down, then swiped at something in a swift, violent motion. I realized she was lighting a match when the smell of burning wax seeped into the hall. My muscles tensed involuntarily; it seemed unsafe to light anything in this old opera house. She bowed her head, remaining silent, as if in prayer.

After a beat, Kristy stood, and I thought she'd noticed me despite the darkness of the hallway. But she stood facing the wall and began to sing, just like she'd taught me during our lesson. Her song was haunting, with a gravitas that felt impossible in modern life. The kind of truth that can only be spoken of ancient things. Though I could not understand the words, I imagined a grand epic of gods and monsters passed down through the centuries, each generation leaving its mark until what remained was both impossibly false and undeniably true.

Kristy sang, louder and louder, and I listened, enthralled. I pictured Xīhé begging Hòuyì to spare the life of her last remaining son, staring into the face of the archer who had murdered her other nine. The White Snake, Bai Suzhen, transforming into a human and marrying Xǔ Xiān, then stealing the immortal herb from Heaven to bring back her husband after accidentally causing his demise. Baigujing realizing Sun Wukong had killed and replaced her demonic friend, and that she would soon follow. Each note sank deep into my bones, the story of each goddess and demon folding itself into my soul. This was beauty and pain and pure, stunning, power.

From somewhere in the distance, a pounding rhythm sounded, growing in volume with Kristy's song. Both were strikingly loud, and yet no one else came to her room.

Goosebumps prickled my flesh as Kristy began to walk, trancelike, toward the mirror, still singing. Like a portal to another realm, it slid open, and she stepped through the frame. I followed, unthinking, moving forward. Drawn to the darkness beyond.

The music cut off as the mirror shut behind Kristy. I felt like someone had torn out a vital piece of me.

The door was locked, but somehow, I knew that if I willed it to open, it would. The Opera House wanted me here. I kept my hand on the handle, putting all of my force into the ask. *Please.* A shock wave pulsed through me, and I heard the latch unclick.

Kristy's room was no longer the sparse bedroom I'd been

in before. Every surface was covered in expensive-looking items. The side table overflowed with bouquets of deep red peonies and Chinese roses, soft pink magnolias and blossoming lotuses. The floor was piled high with gifts, many still crisply wrapped in red and gold. Boxes of tea, fruit baskets, and glass-bottled perfumes littered the remaining spaces.

Barely a week had passed since the night I'd first visited her room. How had all these tokens of admiration accumulated this quickly? They must have been arriving every day.

I waded through the sea of gifts, passing the candle Kristy had lit. It sat on a small red altar, before a photo marked with a lipstick kiss. A little girl sat on the shoulders of a man—in his twenties, probably—both of them laughing. I peered closer. Behind them sat stacks of sheet music and... a violin.

I stared at the instrument.

Yi had translated that article about a violinist who'd disappeared... and left behind a seven-year-old daughter.

And in the teahouse that first morning, Kristy and I had spoken of our dads. *Losing a parent is hard, no matter how it happens. My dad is the reason I started singing. It makes me think of him.*

Holy shit.

I blew out the candle and carved a path to the mirror. When I reached it, I felt around the side, right around where it had opened last time, and pulled.

The mirror didn't budge.

I frowned, pulling harder in case it was stuck.

It still wouldn't move.

I leaned closer to inspect the side. No keyhole, no latch, no gap at all; as if wall and mirror were fused. I kept my hand on the seam, willing it open the way I had with Kristy's door. Nothing happened.

Then I realized she had shown me the way.

I stood before the mirror and began to sing, echoing Kristy. It shouldn't have been possible when I was unfamiliar with her melody, when I didn't understand the words, and yet they came to me. My voice carried further than it should have, each note reverberating off the walls of the Opera House.

Finally, the mirror opened.

As before, the corridor was dark and full of cobwebs. The air felt thick and cloying, like I was breathing in a swamp. I moved as quickly as I could on the rough stone floor.

Further into the passageway, the smell of roasting meat wafted its way into my nose. What the hell? The scent filled my taste buds with the savor of flesh and blood. I felt the tantalizing prickle of Tang Sanzang's cheek stubble on my tongue, the chewiness of his skin between my teeth. Saliva filled my mouth.

Distracted, I tripped, landing hard on slimy stone. Something skittered and I squeaked, pushing myself up off the floor as a wormy pink rat tail disappeared into the darkness. My heart pounded in my ears as I brushed chunks of dirt off my hands and clothes. For a moment, I questioned what the hell I was doing in this disgusting cave.

But by then, the need to know pulled stronger than reason. I thought of Kristy kissing the photo of her father—who had disappeared all those years ago—and walking through the mirror. Something was happening tonight, and I couldn't miss it. I was past the point of no return. I needed to find out where this road led.

I continued on the path until I reached a steep set of stairs leading downward. Thick, roiling mist filled the air, clouding the glimmering light originating from somewhere below. The stone steps were unevenly cut, and there was no railing. I used the wall to steady myself, grimacing when my fingers brushed a layer of slick, fuzzy mold.

As I descended, my eyes adjusted until I found myself looking down into a vast chamber lit by flickering candles. It was like a bloated, warped version of the one I'd fallen into several nights earlier; the one where I—Aili—had faced my death. Back then, it had been more of a room, less of a cave.

I thought of how Wei had described Huihuang Opera House; imagined this secret room growing monstrous over the years. My gaze landed on a curtained corner mostly shrouded in shadow, and I felt my face grow hot with the memory of Aili's lips on my neck, her hand between my legs. Sets of stalactites and stalagmites had grown partially over it, like a ribcage protecting a beating heart. It had changed but it was still here, all these decades later.

From the distance, a set of disembodied voices traveled up. I snuck down the wide stairs more cautiously, trying to make out details of the conversation.

"Soon enough, you'll have everything you could ever want." Though the voice wasn't loud, it resonated; the air vibrated with each word, like the whole cave was speaking. I knew that voice like I knew my own; breathy whispers in my ear every night in our secret place; songs on stage every night while I danced behind her. But there was more to it, too. It was Aili if she were in command of an army. Aili with the eyes of an entire theater on her. Aili infused with something deeper, older.

"I know what you did to my father." The second voice was soft and human and familiar, too. Kristy.

Something about their words felt wrong, but I couldn't pinpoint why.

Aili cackled lightly, an almost pleasant sound. *"He made a fair bargain. As will you. I can see it in your hungry eyes. You've had a taste. You won't choose obscurity now."*

Realization dawned. I understood everything with the ease of someone listening to a conversation in their native tongue. But they spoke in Mandarin.

My mind reeled as I continued my descent. Famous musicians missing once every decade. Aili's dancer, Kristy's father. A singer whose story I had yet to learn. A bargain extended.

I reached the bottom of the stairs and crept toward the voices, still cloaked in shadow. Various dark shapes lined the pathway, both strange and fitting in the eerie cavern. As I neared, each object rendered itself more clearly. I reached out to touch some of them as I passed. A black cauldron, surface rough and cold, sat beside a shelf of spices. Just beyond them, strips of jerky hung from a tiered drying rack. These hadn't been in the chamber before; I felt sure of it.

I stopped when I reached the edge of the shadows. By the light of countless candles, I spotted two figures on a twisted facsimile of the auditorium stage; peeling paint and rotting wood, eyes gouged out of the carved animals. A black beetle crawled out of a lion's mouth and scurried up the post; in the shadows at the back of the stage, something squeaked.

Kristy, still in costume, faced down the White Bone Demon, both of them visible only in profile.

I drew in a breath. Everything about Baigujing looked too realistic, like a creature straight out of legend. Where Kristy's opera headdress was full of pretty embroidery and white polka-dotted pompoms, Baigujing's was made of twisted steel and shrunken skulls. Instead of two long feathers growing from the sides of her headdress, a pair of impossibly long, insect-like tendrils twitched as she spoke. She was pale and bony, and her face was oily white, the hue too solid and realistic to be the kind of makeup Kristy wore onstage.

She was Aili, but she was more, too. A warped, reborn version of the performer. I remembered begging the Opera House to keep Xueli safe; the promise made in return.

I'll do anything for you.

The pieces began clicking into place. Aili, assaulted in the middle of playing Baigujing, all terror and anger and desperation as she found herself trapped with a violent man. After he'd taken what he wanted from her, he'd left her for dead.

The Opera House could not protect Aili from death, but it had done what it could. After ten years without opera, Huihuang had come alive again with *Sun Wukong San Da Baigujing*. I could see it clearly as a memory: Aili, bleeding out in costume, fusing with the Demon—a demon who had clawed her way back from death three times.

Together, they had shown me all the pieces.

Kristy stared down Baigujing. *"I wanted to understand why my father would choose this."*

"And do you?" Baigujing's lips parted in a grin, showing off stained teeth.

Kristy bared her teeth in return. *"I do. You prey on the young, on the desperate. You're as bad as the man who murdered you."*

Baigujing snarled and leapt forward, grabbing Kristy by the throat. *"He and I are nothing alike!"* Her voice was no longer beautiful; it was gravelly, full of menace. *"Your father made a choice. Your love of music and everything you have comes from him, from me. You should be grateful I extend you the same offer."*

I lurched forward, stopping only when Baigujing released Kristy, who coughed and clutched her throat.

"You want this as much as he did."

Kristy nodded, looking down.

Baigujing's voice rose, her eyes grown manic. She spoke with a practiced rhythm, like a fae thing forced to lay out the terms for a human who had wandered onto her land. *"Cut out your tongue, and the bargain is sealed. No one will know, save you and I. For ten years, you will speak and sing through my power alone, growing as famous as you wish. When your time is up, you will return here. I promise your death will be quick; what I do with your body will be no concern of yours."* She smiled wider, eyes glinting as she showed off serrated teeth.

I stared at the creature Deng Aili had become. A part of me understood. Sympathized, even.

But there was an insinuation behind her words, her sharp smile. And that persistent smell of roasted meat.

At the end of ten years, she meant to eat Kristy's corpse.

Kristy looked up with an unreadable expression. She reached out, and Aili placed a knife in her hand, blade sharp.

Kristy lifted the knife, and I understood that she would cut out her own tongue; trade away most of her life for a few years in the limelight. Kristy, who everyone admired. Kristy, who had a rich fiancé and enough talent to join the opera troupe even before she'd had a taste of Baigujing's powers. Kristy, who already had everything she could ever need.

I screamed as I ran forward and climbed onto the stage.

Baigujing let out a hiss, turning toward me, but Kristy didn't turn, didn't flinch. She plunged the knife into the

White Bone Demon's chest. *"I'm going to make sure you can never hurt anyone again."*

Baigujing crumpled to the ground with a choked gasp.

Kristy leaned over her, pulled out the knife, screamed, and stabbed her again. And again.

I grabbed Kristy's arm. Reflexively, she yanked it back, elbowing me hard. I stumbled backward, knocking over the table behind me. The lit candles tumbled to the ground.

The flames caught quickly, filling the air with smoke. Fire found Baigujing's rack of dried meat strips which charred and blackened, thickening the smoky air.

I gagged, realizing they must be the remains of Baigujing's last victim, preserved for slow consumption.

Kristy was still on her knees, staring at Baigujing's fallen body as if she couldn't tear her eyes away.

"Kristy!" I shouted. Then a coughing fit overtook me.

My words seemed to snap her out of her trance. Kristy whirled around and opened her mouth to reply, but then she began coughing too. I could feel the sweat forming on my skin, my eyeballs drying out like the times I'd stepped too near a campfire. We needed to get the hell out of here.

Coughing, Kristy and I clung to one another as we stumbled away from the woman—the creature—she'd just killed.

As we turned our backs to Baigujing, burning on her pyre, unease filled me. Though I'd watched Kristy stab her repeatedly, I still couldn't quite believe the demon was gone. She felt like a force of nature; too powerful to be killed as any mortal might be. Her desire for life, for vengeance; her white-hot anger. Where would it all go without the vessel of her body to contain it?

There was no time to dwell on it.

I let myself glance back for only a moment. Without Kristy blocking the way, I could see the demon's face in its entirety, shocked expression aglow in the light of the flames. Half of Baigujing's face was bone-white and unblemished. The other half was carved up, a gaping hole exposing a jaw full of rotted teeth sprouting from gray-ish red muscles.

And then my survival instinct roared to life. Kristy was moving too slowly, seemingly in shock; I grabbed her hand and did my best to pull her forward. Smoke burned my eyes, but I was relentless. We were *not* going to die there.

By the time we reached the stone staircase, Kristy's shock had faded enough for us to run up, together. I wasn't thinking about the Demon anymore; I wasn't thinking about anything but the mirror ahead. All we had to do was get out of this chamber, away from the flames, and we'd have a chance at safety, at life, at all those precious years. Bright, beautiful futures sat just on the horizon—they were ours for the keeping, if only we could reach them.

When we neared the top of the stairs, Kristy was suddenly yanked back, as if something had grabbed her by the waist.

Her hand slipped out of mine, and she fell down the steps. The fire hadn't yet caught up to us, but she screamed and writhed as though she were burning alive. As if she were being punished for trying to leave the chamber. The Opera House wasn't ready to let her go.

Frantic, I shouted her name, my throat growing hoarse as I watched her tumble into the inferno.

I couldn't save her.

I made the only choice I had left. I ran the rest of the way up the stairs, up the smoky corridor, heart heavy as I burst through the open mirror into Kristy's room. I collapsed to the ground in a coughing fit, unshed tears burning behind my eyes. Alarms blared, and the air was filled with panicked shouts, and I willed myself to get up, to keep going. The fire would spread, and I wasn't safe yet.

But my limbs felt sluggish and heavy; my body refused to move.

Someone shouted for Kèlín—Kristy—and then strong arms were lifting me up, dragging me out of the room, and I tried to tell them about Kristy, but all that came out of my mouth was a relentless coughing fit that tore up my throat, leaving me raw and ragged.

CHAPTER 15

When we emerged from the smoke, I saw it was Siquan who had found and carried me out of Kristy's room. He set me down. I wanted to thank him, but I still couldn't speak. My lungs felt like they were on fire.

"Kelin?" His eyes were wide with intensity.

I shook my head.

And then a car door was thrown open and Mom was hurtling toward me. She wrapped me in a tight hug, fat tears pouring down her cheeks. She sobbed my name over and over, alternating between running her fingers over my face and clutching me so hard I could barely catch my breath. Siquan vanished into the crowd, and then it was just Mom and me.

My throat was hoarse, and no matter how much water I downed, I was still parched. I tried to tell Mom I was okay, but that launched another coughing fit. Mom stroked my hair, crying as she told me to save my voice. Promising we'd talk later.

We watched the fiery glow of Huihuang Opera House die down as the emergency sprinkler system—installed with the recent renovations—extinguished the flames. I wasn't sure if the sting in my eyes was from the aftereffects of the smoke or my relief that the three-hundred-year-old building had survived, if badly scathed. I didn't want to be responsible for the theater's death.

∽

I find myself hesitant, now, to share what came next. I worry that even with all I've explained, you won't understand. You've never had to lie awake, listening to the sound of someone you love being thrown against the wall of the next room over, wondering if you should run outside and tell a stranger or if that would make everything worse. You've never felt the body-wracking chills, the bone-weary exhaustion, the constant distraction of an empty stomach. Nor have you known the loneliness of being forced to leave a life behind over and over again.

Sometimes, I envy you. I know it's petty and pointless, that you were no more an engineer in the circumstances you were born into than I in mine. That I should be glad your hardships are less. That you had the chance to grow up with a full pantry and lasting friendships and a mother with the time and the energy to love you.

I am glad, most days.

But there are other days.

I tell you these things that I should probably keep to myself because I want you to know me. All of me.

I can feel the call again; it grows harder to resist. And so, I will end these ruminations and finish my tale.

∞

That night, Mom and I sat on the floor of Wei's living room, leaning against the couch. Wei was out dealing with the aftermath of the disaster. It was just the two of us. I had made it out; Mom and I were safe, and Kristy was not. Even now, after seeing that expression on her face right before the flames consumed her, I couldn't believe she was gone. She'd felt invincible.

My throat still hurt, so Mom brought me a pen and paper to write with. We wrapped ourselves up in the thin blankets Wei had left for us and huddled close. Mom took a sip of tea, clearing her throat.

"Megan... I'm sorry."

I thought of Mom yanking me back from the tunnel behind the mirror. The way she had always divided our cleaning duties so I was never responsible for the performers' rooms. Her youthful smile, captured in the article about the Opera House. I began to write.

You knew.

Mom worried her lip, and I could tell she was deciding whether to lie, so I picked up the pen again.

Please tell me the truth.

Slowly, she acquiesced. "It all started with a boy." She saw my scowl and sighed. "Megan, I'm not naïve. I know what you think of my relationships."

I wanted to snipe, but I was afraid she'd stop talking. And she was finally going to tell me *something*.

"I was seventeen and running away with him seemed like a good idea at the time. My parents were hell-bent on my getting a college degree in a safe career track. And there were... other problems. I couldn't imagine the kind of life they wanted for me. I needed my freedom. My boyfriend was in the show. He got me a job selling tickets."

BF = Wei?

If Wei had told me the truth, he wasn't. But I wanted to hear it from Mom. I wanted to see how much she'd tell me, finally.

Mom laughed. "No, though I met Wei around then. He was years younger than me, the son of the theater owner, and I could tell he was smitten. But he was just a child. I lived and worked at Huihuang Opera House, and I heard the call of Baigujing." She watched me for a reaction.

I heard it too.

Her voice trembled the way it did when she'd first found me after the fire. "You were down there in her chamber, weren't you?" I nodded. I squeezed my eyes shut as I thought, again, of Kristy. Mom let out a soft sob, tears streaming down her face as she hugged me again. She whispered into my hair, "I almost made the bargain. I wanted to be talented. To be famous."

Gently, I pulled away from her and wrote again.

Why didn't you?

Mom wiped the tears from her face. "Because I wanted to do everything. To see the world. Because ten years wasn't enough time to fit in all the adventures I dreamt of. And once I had you, I knew I'd made the right choice. If I'd taken that bargain, I would have left you alone in the world."

Mom's words wrapped around my heart. I couldn't imagine a life without her. One small change in the events leading up to that moment, and we could have lost one another in the fire. That kind of loss felt unfathomable.

I recalled Kristy kissing the photo of her and her father; her low, angry words as she stabbed Baigujing. *I'm going to make sure you can never hurt anyone again.*

He'd vanished when she was seven, leaving her wondering all those years. For the first time, I thought of her joining this troupe; it had been no coincidence. She'd come here to learn what had happened to her father, to find Baigujing, to get closure.

Mom gave me another hug before continuing. "I know it's been hard at times... but look at the lives we've led! How many teenagers can say they've lived in an opera house, like you and me? How many people have had the chance to live in as many cities as we have?"

I felt my frustration take root. She was doing what she always did—painting our lives in a rosy light. I wrapped the blanket tighter, wishing its flimsy warmth could fill the hollowness her words left me with. I was tempted to walk out then. She'd learned nothing.

Of all things, it was my conversation with Wei that stopped me. *You know what her father was like.*

I could imagine her as a kid, telling herself pretty stories about her life as she hid from her dad. Maybe that was why she was like this; she had grown up hiding the truth from herself. Maybe it wasn't me she was trying to convince.

"I thought I could keep you safe." Mom started crying again. "I see now that I should never have brought you here, no matter how bad... no matter what. I'm sorry, Megan. We'll sleep here tonight and find a new place to go in the morning. I promise."

I'd been wanting to hear those words since we arrived. To my own surprise, I shook my head and began writing.

I want to stay here.

She stared at me. "Really?"

I thought about what I was saying. Was this a terrible idea?

I didn't think Wei or the Opera House were permanent solutions for us, but maybe they could be part of a new beginning. A true fresh start—not Mom's idea of one, but mine. She'd finally admitted to knowing about Baigujing, and she'd made a passing reference to problems at home while growing up.

Maybe.

Yes, I'm sure.

"I don't think we can stay in the Opera House anymore. The fire..."

Here. Wei's.

For the first time since the fire, Mom smiled at me. "Okay. Let's do that."

Despite everything that had happened, my heart felt fuller than it had in years. I could picture our lives ahead. Wei would be out a lot, overseeing the Opera House restoration. Mom and I would help clean; or maybe, with us moving into his house, we could finally end the façade that Mom and I were here to work. He'd still say annoying things, but he wouldn't be around all the time. Mom and I would have time to ourselves. We could bus around the city, visit the places from her memory. She could tell me what had changed; what hadn't.

Maybe I could get to the bottom of what happened between her and her family, why she never spoke to them. Maybe I could even meet whatever relatives we had left.

I pictured going to try street food with a distant cousin, and my eyes filled with tears. Mom saw them and took my hands in hers, squeezing tight.

Her sleeve fell, revealing her pale wrist. There, in the center, was a faint purple blotch.

Shaped like a thumbprint.

The world dropped out from under me.

I felt myself pulled back, hurtled into a memory forever seared into my mind. Mom, eyes black, skin mottled with bruises, lying motionless on the hardwood floor, surrounded by shards of a shattered Ming vase.

I couldn't breathe.

Mom's face drained of color. "Megan, it's nothing! He just grabbed my arm a little too hard while we were out, he didn't mean anything by it."

How many times had I heard those words? How many times had I seen where they led?

I had sat in his office that afternoon, asking him about Mom and the Opera House. Accepting the olive branches he'd extended. He'd told me how much he loved her, and then he'd done this.

"We can still stay!" Mom faltered. "Or we can go. If you want, we can leave."

All those little moments I'd pictured with Mom shriveled like dying flowers. If we left, we would never have any of them. We would never break the cycle. We would always be running.

I forced myself to write.

Where?

"We'll find somewhere," she said. "We always find somewhere."

I thought about all the places we'd been; all the places we'd left.

Mom had known about Baigujing. She'd been afraid of the danger the demon posed to me, but as always, there was no good option when you had to balance food, shelter, and safety. I'd thought she just hated cleaning bathrooms; but she must have been trying to keep me away from the mirror in Kristy's bedroom. That night she'd found me there... she'd been worried. But she had to keep Wei happy. She was stretched so thin.

We had nowhere left in the world to go, and she and I both knew it.

Within me, fury rose. I'd spent my whole life suppressing its spark, directing my frustration at Mom's flightiness, at her terrible romantic choices.

But she wasn't the problem.

I thought of the nurses giving me and Mom sympathetic glances. Of the man who'd hurt her there, at the hospital, talking and laughing with the doctors. He'd been important enough for them to look the other way. Rich, powerful men always got what they wanted.

We couldn't go on like this, but neither could we stay.

I'm tired. Talk in AM?

"Of course." Mom looked relieved. She hugged me tight before disappearing into another room. She came back with pillows and blankets. The big, plush couch was a comfy enough mattress. She tucked me in, and I closed my eyes, forcing back tears.

Mom brushed my hair out of my face and sang a lullaby, like I was a child again. Internally, my rage was hardening into a steely certainty, but I kept it reined in tight.

At last, Mom made herself a makeshift bed on the floor and laid down. It was ages before she drifted off. I waited long enough for her to fall into deep sleep.

While I lay there, thoughts swirled through my mind along with images, vibrant and too stubborn to leave me alone. Baigujing pressing the knife into Kristy's hand. Kristy stabbing her, screaming accusations. The gaping hole in Baigujing's face, tongue missing, as we left her to burn.

I looked at Mom. Her lips quivered with each indrawn breath. Wear lines and faint white scars marked the trials she'd faced.

Careful not to wake Mom, I got up and rifled through her purse until I found her old copy of *Xiyouji*. She was still asleep when I opened the door and stepped out into the night, book tucked under my arm.

Wei lived three blocks from Huihuang Opera House. I took my time walking along the cobblestone streets, thinking about the story I'd read. Baigujing had clawed her way out of her grave three times. Each would-be-fatal blow had only made her craving for youth and flesh stronger than ever.

She was a survivor.

The air was still smoky from the fire. By then, the crowds had dispersed. The streets weren't empty—I doubted they ever were in the heart of Beijing—but it was peaceful. No one stopped me.

I hated where my thoughts went, but I couldn't stop my mind from racing ahead. Kristy had been kind to me, had treated me like a jiějie might treat her mèimei. But now she was gone, and she'd left a gaping hole her troupe would be looking to fill.

As I approached the Opera House, I stopped to look up, to take in its façade. Parts of it were charred black, but the golden phoenix stood tall, wings wide and welcoming. There was tape around the front blocking it off, yet no one seemed to be looking quite my way when I slipped beneath and climbed up the steps. No one noticed when I opened the red door and stepped inside.

At the auditorium, I stopped, staring up at the stage. I could imagine myself front and center, singing my heart out. I would have a dressing room like Kristy's, where I'd store gifts from enraptured theatergoers. But I'd ignore them all and head straight for the house where Mom and I lived.

My eyes closed for a moment, savoring the image. Dad had always said my dreams were too small. I'd wanted the lead in my school play. To him, I was meant for Broadway.

I pictured a buttercup-yellow house in a modest neighborhood with a garden full of flowers. A space just big enough to keep us shielded from the world. Mom and I would paint the door amethyst, her favorite color. I'd give her the biggest room—a place where she could heal, where she could grow old. Two bedrooms, with a porch that looked out onto a quiet neighborhood, and a bunk bed in my room for Yi to stay in when she visited. A place that belonged to me and Mom because we finally had money to call our own.

I didn't know if Mom would ever understand that to me, ten years of security was worth more than a lifetime of pretenses.

As I headed for Kristy's former room, my fingers flexed, the weight of an imaginary knife against my palm, the curl of my hand around an invisible hilt. I sang to the mirror, and no part of me was surprised when it opened.

⌒

Inside the chamber, everything was blackened. My steps kicked up a layer of ash that stung my eyes and nose, but I kept going. I braced myself to see a body on the steps, burnt and unrecognizable. Yet, there was none.

Did I begin to suspect, then?

I remembered Kristy's scream as she was yanked back into the fire—the sound that would haunt me for years to come.

And I wondered.

As I neared the bottom of the stairs, I saw Baigujing. She was no longer the regal, self-assured creature I'd seen. She was a twisted, awkward thing, crouched low over a still form. The chamber was dead silent, save the sound of smacking lips.

"Aili?" I whispered as I approached. My throat was still tender.

She turned to hiss at me, head covered in malformed skulls, tendrils limp and gray. Her mouth was bright red with gore, and when she grinned wide, strings of wet meat hung down from between her teeth. Her cheeks were intact. Whole.

Not Aili.

I stared in shock at the once-beautiful face. I'd so envied her poise, her grace, the way she'd carried herself with straight-backed confidence. Mere hours earlier, I'd watched her captivate a full theater with her voice. I'd held her hand as we ran from the fire, up the staircase toward safety.

Now, her skin was sallow and chalky white.

Kristy turned back to her feast, the sounds louder and wetter than before, and I winced; it was so unlike the delicate way she'd eaten the few meals we'd shared. I turned away for a moment, heart pounding.

I didn't need to study the body lying face up on the stone floor; didn't need to stare into those sightless eyes to know whom Kristy consumed.

Too well, I could imagine Aili hunched over her lover's body all those years ago—her first bargain offered and accepted. Next, Chen Guoliang, leaving his child behind as he became Aili's second victim. Then, the singer who was Aili's third.

Now, it was Aili's turn to provide sustenance to the new Demon of the Opera.

I ran my tongue along my teeth, taking the time to savor each distinct bump and ridge of enamel against the rough muscle.

Then I forced myself to turn back before I could lose my nerve.

Kristy handed me the knife, slick with blood, and I licked my lips before tucking my tongue back in one last time.

I would miss it when it was gone.

CHAPTER 16

And so, I am back here in Beijing at the end of things, in the newly built luxury hotel facing Huihuang Opera House. Pausing once in a while to stare out the window at the place where it all began.

When it finally comes time to face the music, everyone wonders the same thing: do you regret it?

The most honest answer I can give is that I am not sure.

Regret is a luxury granted to those with choices. It would be easy to regret what I am about to lose now that I've lived in fame and privilege and comfort for a decade. Now that I know what it is to stand before a crowd and enthrall them with the voice of Baigujing. Now that I've felt the joy of returning home to find our mom with your dad, cooking dinner together, Mom bursting into a fit of giggles as she wipes a spot of sauce off his nose.

But without the choices I made, she would not have met him, would not have had you.

Maybe it's not a difficult question to answer, after all.

Still, I wish there could have been another way. In the years after I met with the demon, I wrestled with how I'd avoid the mistakes of the past. I swore to myself I would not do what Kristy's father did. That I would not have a child only to leave them behind.

And I kept my promise. But Mom did not make a promise, did not know or did not care what her choices would mean for me.

On dark nights, when I lie awake remembering the lives she and I once led, I wonder if she had you because of my bargain. If you are my replacement; so that if your father leaves her someday, she will not live out her days alone.

As much as I love you, you are one more thing I cannot forgive her for.

How I long to watch you grow up. To teach you to sing my favorite songs and take you with me on a tour around the world. To wrap you in a huge hug the first time someone at school makes you cry. To listen to you tell me of your dreams for the future while we sip hot cocoa from matching mugs. To give you everything I never had, growing up.

Instead, I leave you with this poor substitute built of words and memories, this shell of an older sister.

I can resist the pull no longer. Baigujing's bone-white face and hungry eyes fill my waking mind; her song invades my dreams. Every breath I take imbues me with longing, with the desperate, all-consuming need to return to the Opera House.

I have imagined these last moments a thousand times. Our reunion after all these years; the way we would soon become one.

As dusk falls, I will call you and Mom one last time to say goodnight. After we hang up, I will make my way to the Opera House, retracing the path I walked all those years ago. Wind my way through Huihuang's familiar halls and through the mirror, down to where the White Bone Demon has waited ten long years for my return. From atop her stage, she will reach down, offering me a pale hand.

And I will accept.

THE END.

AFTERWORD

I was nine years old the first time my dad took me to see a musical. Though many of my memories from that age have faded with the fickleness of recall, this one lingers. I remember being blown away by the elaborate costuming, the grand gothic set trappings, the musical score, and above all, the absolute feat of nature that was the performers' singing, their transcendent voices filling the theater with a kind of emotional verve that left me wishing I could relive those moments ad infinitum.

The musical was *The Phantom of the Opera*, and I've since seen the live show twice more, watched the 2004 film countless times, and read the novel by Gaston Leroux. It is to *Phantom* and everyone involved in its production that I credit both my enduring love of musicals (something my dad and I share) and my initial spark of interest in all things gothic.

Hop forward seven or so years to my sixteenth birthday, when my family visited China for the first time. While my mom grew up in Taiwan, my dad the Philippines, I was born and raised in the United States. Like that first time watching *Phantom*, stepping foot in China was an otherworldly experience, but for an entirely different reason—it was the first time I'd ever blended in with the crowds around me. It was also the first time I'd been in a place where nearly everyone spoke in Chinese languages—including Mandarin, with which I continue to have a complicated relationship.

We spent two weeks in China, traveling to four major cities, one of which was Beijing. Just south of Tiananmen Square —a place filled with history, including the infamous 1989 massacre—I was introduced to Chinese opera through a performance held at Liyuan Theatre.

Several days later in Xi'an, I experienced another performance-art-related moment I would never forget. As part of our guided tour, we attended a combined dinner and show. There, at one of many round banquet tables, we sat among countless other guests, everyone feasting on the same delicious spread as we enjoyed a lively performance.

Halfway through, a group of costumed performers began carrying a cake down the aisle with great pomp and circumstance while singing "Happy Birthday" in Mandarin. I was surprised that someone else there shared my birthday, and I said something along those lines to my mom. She merely smiled.

Unbeknownst to me, she had arranged a surprise

with our tour guide. I watched in complete disbelief as the performers turned and headed straight for our table, where they set down the cake. They lit the lotus flower cake topper and it bloomed, the tip of each unfurled petal a tiny, glowing candle. Then they gently nudged me to stand, before asking my assistance to unsheathe a dramatically large, curved sword. Together, we cut the cake while strangers around us cheered and snapped photos.

Between all these occurrences, it should, perhaps, be no surprise at all that years later, the concept for *Demon Song* showed up raring for my attention. It began as the seed of an idea: what if Meg Giry, daughter of the opera house madame in *Phantom*, and best friend to Christine Daaé, had the chance to tell her story? I had long wondered how Meg felt about the sudden spotlight on her friend... and what her relationship with her mother must be like, given the complexity of Madame Giry's character and situation.

Around that time, I also purchased a copy of *Chinese Opera: Images and Stories* by Siu Wang-Ngai and Peter Lovrick. I was enthralled by the beautiful illustrations and detailed descriptions. Before then, I hadn't known how varied and storied an art form Chinese opera is.

My musings about *The Phantom of the Opera* and Chinese opera swirled together into what I thought, at first blush, was a short story. But as I researched— everything from reading accounts of the Cultural Revolution, to watching videos of a

Beijing opera star teach a Chinese American extreme athlete to play the infamous Monkey King—it quickly became apparent that *Demon Song* wanted to be more. And so, through many rounds of revisions, it has grown into the novella it is now.

My main character, Megan, isn't me, but there's a lot of me and my experiences in her story—her struggles with language and identity (in multiple regards), her patchy knowledge of Chinese classics and mythology, and her yearning to know more, to be more. For me, as for Megan, theaters, performing arts, and family will always be inextricably tied.

Demon Song is my love letter to the enchanting gothic tale that first captured my attention all those years ago, wrapped in an envelope of Chinese opera and mythology. Thank you for reading.

ACKNOWLEDGMENTS

In the four years since I first began working on the tale that would become *Demon Song*, the manuscript has gone through countless iterations. Along the way, I've been incredibly fortunate in receiving an abundance of support from many sources.

To my agent, Jennifer Azantian—thank you for being an unwavering champion for my books, always. Your supportiveness, expertise, and trustworthiness are truly unmatched. I'm proud to have you as a partner in my writing endeavors.

To my editor, Daniel Carpenter—your keen editorial eye helped me strengthen Megan's story more than I would have thought possible. Thank you for your reliability, your enthusiasm, your hard work, and most of all, your genuine care.

To the entire team at Titan, including Charlotte Kelly, Katharine Carroll, Amy Hack, Caitlin Storer, Simon Mann, Dan Coxon and Paul Simpson—thank you for all the work you've put into this book at every step along the way. It has been a joy working with such a kind, enthusiastic, and capable team.

I was fortunate enough to have a number of beta readers and early supporters of this book. To Sophie Normil, Jena Brown, CG Drews, Clare Edge, Jill Tew, Leah Ning, Miche Tang, Maraia Bonsignore, Ben Baxter, Zhui Ning Chang, Lee Murray, Alex Woodroe, and Matt Blairstone—thank you for your encouragement and insight. It means a ton to me that you've all taken the time out of your busy lives to read my stories.

Thank you also to the following for your friendship, advice, encouragement, and commiseration: Isa Agajanian, Rosiee Thor, Courtney Gould, Megan Lally, Laura Cranehill, Caitlin Starling, Ellie Thomas, Ai Jiang, Marie Croke, Rebecca E. Treasure, Marissa van Uden, Anna Madden, Amy Henry Robinson, Beth Dawkins, Samir Sirk Morató, Sasha Brown, Cormack Baldwin, Nichole L. Lightner, Kay Vaindal, Ende Mac, Miel MacRae, Mackenzie Moody, Shari Beltran, Stephanie Cheng, Cara Klein, Carina Saal, Sana Shams, Gagan Kaur, Mercy Gonzáles, Joséphine Kühn, Soren Dominguez, Elise DuBois, Erin Hartel, Christine Lee, Amanda Askew, Sadie Hartmann, Ashley Saywers, A.D. Sui, Teresa Weitz, Thamires Vitello, Carolyn Brooks, Carl Laviolette, Nikki Brown, Hazelmae Overturf, Cameron Overturf, Catherine Yu, Frances Lu-Pai Ippolito, and Ashley Deng. Thank you also to all the friends I've made through Bookstagram, Discord, Slack, local groups, and elsewhere—your support of my writing journey has meant the world to me.

Tal, Mom, Dad, Corbin, Collin, Nora, Carol, Bob, Patrick, and Alex—thank you for the continual encouragement, watching the kids so I have time to write, and for your patience as I talk endlessly about books. To my kiddos, B, K, and L—watching you grow up is both a joy and an inspiration. I'm forever grateful to have such a supportive family. Love you all.

Dad, you taught me to dream big, work hard, and never settle—all of which led me down this path. Thank you.

And to everyone who blurbed, reviewed, read, bought, shared, featured, or recommended my books and stories—you continue to help make my dream career possible. A million times, thank you.

ABOUT THE AUTHOR

Kelsea Yu is a Taiwanese Chinese American writer who is eternally enthusiastic about sharks and appreciates a good ghost story. Her novella, *Bound Feet*, was a Shirley Jackson Award finalist, and her debut novel, *It's Only a Game*, won a Children's Book Council Award. Dozens of Kelsea's short stories and essays appear in *Nightmare*, *Apex*, *PseudoPod*, *Clarkesworld*, various award-winning anthologies, podcasts, and elsewhere. Find her on Instagram as @anovelescape or visit her website kelseayu.com. Kelsea lives in Portland, Oregon, with her husband, children, and a pile of art supplies.

For more fantastic fiction, author events,
exclusive excerpts, competitions, limited editions and more

VISIT OUR WEBSITE
titanbooks.com

LIKE US ON FACEBOOK
facebook.com/titanbooks

FOLLOW US ON TWITTER AND INSTAGRAM
@TitanBooks

EMAIL US
readerfeedback@titanemail.com